HER ORC KING

A MONSTER FANTASY ROMANCE

BLACK BEAR CLAN

ZOE ASHWOOD

Line Edit by Emmy Ellis

Proofreading by Lori Parks

Cover by White Book Designs

Created with Vellum

A LETTER TO MY READERS

Hello, dear reader!

I'm so happy you picked up this story! *Her Orc King* is the first book in the *Black Bear Clan* series and it's a M/F fantasy orc romance. All the books in this series are standalones and each features a happy ending for that couple.

Want a free orc story? Get *Her Orc Mate* today - if you're reading this in paperback form or can't access the link, email me at zoe@zoeashwood.com!

I put the content warnings for the series on my blog in case you want to check them out - but didn't want to list them here so I don't spoil anything for you. I want you to have a safe reading experience!

. . .

Enjoy the story!
  xo, Zoe

CHAPTER
ONE

If you told me two weeks ago I'd be kidnapped, sold at auction, and dragged to the orc territory deep in the forests of Bellhaven, I'd call you crazy and distance myself posthaste.

But here I am. Trapped in a wagon, trussed up while two massive orc guards sit on either side of me, their faces grim. I'm probably well on my way to becoming a sex slave, and I need to find a way out of here. Now.

"I promise I won't try to run again," I plead, doing my best impression of a meek damsel in distress. "Or stab you."

The older of the two guards, the one with a deeply scarred face called Ozork, scowls at me. "That's what you said the last time."

"And the time before that," adds the younger orc, Neekar, grinning as if receiving a stab wound in the thigh is something to be proud of.

They've been remarkably calm about my escape attempts. Ever since they purchased me like a cow at the market in Ultrup, they've treated me kindly—even though their idea of kindness was giving me an additional blanket to wrap myself against the night cold as they forced me to sleep on the ground by the campfire.

They'd ordered me to bathe in the first stream we'd come across after leaving town, probably because I smelled horrendously bad after spending a week in the slave barracks in Ultrup. But they hadn't given me any privacy, and I couldn't wash properly in the freezing river swollen from the melting snow. So now I'm dirty, still dressed in the simple wool gown I was wearing when the band of slavers kidnapped me. I can't even smell myself anymore, so I think my odor must be terrible.

That hasn't prevented the orcs in this party from sniffing me. Every warrior has come close to me at some point and taken a deep whiff of my hair, the skin on my wrists, my neck. I'd endured it all, petrified. I'd thought they were smelling me to determine if I was tasty or something even more nefarious, but all they'd done was grunt and move off again.

There's no telling what these creatures have planned for me. I've heard all the horrific tales about orcs and their lairs deep in the mountains. But I won't stop trying to escape. I'll keep attempting different tactics until something sticks.

"How long before we get there?" I ask instead of protesting again. I make my voice whiny and trembling. If they think I'm weak, they might let their guard down and allow me to escape.

"Not long," is the curt reply I get.

I sit straighter. Up until this moment, every reply had been, "Stop talking," or "You'll know when we get there."

So we're nearing our destination.

We passed through an orc village several miles ago, and one of the cloth-covered wagons in our convoy stopped there—along with at least two of the human passengers who had been bought at auction with me. There were four of us—an elderly woman with silver hair, a middle-aged man, and a boy perhaps twelve years old.

"What happened to the child?" I ask my guards.

I haven't dared ask before, because the answer might be too horrifying to bear, but I owe my fellow captives that small mercy. To learn of their fate and maybe send word to their families if I can manage to sneak away. I would have hoped that the others would do the same for me, only I have no one to notify. The people who might come searching for me would definitely not have my best interests at heart.

"Why do you want to know?" asks the older orc, glowering fiercely.

I grind my teeth, then force myself to reply in a calm voice. "Because he's young. He was so scared. Why did you even buy him?"

The two orcs exchange a long look. Then the younger one shrugs as if to say, *Might as well tell her*.

"He is being returned to his village," the older orc says. "Two of our best warriors are escorting him home."

Oh.

I blink, surprised at the answer. I'd been picturing child slave labor and other horrible things, but if what they're saying is true, the boy was likely saved by them.

"Will you let *me* go and escort me back h—to my village?"

I almost choke on that word. *Home*. I haven't known a true home in years, and I don't know what I'd find if these orcs ever did return me to our small settlement.

A grueling job, debt, and a man all too willing to forgive it… with the right incentive.

I shudder at the thought and focus instead on glaring at the orcs.

"No," says Ozork. "You're staying with us."

"But why?" Even to my own ears my voice sounds whiny, yet I can't help myself.

Neekar opens his mouth as if to say something, but his companion kicks his shin to shut him up. They glare at each other for a moment, then stare out the back of the wagon.

All right, so there's definitely a purpose to my being dragged through these forests and hills. Whatever fate awaits me there, I'm sure it's not good.

I squeeze my knees together, a sense of foreboding washing over me. There isn't much use a twenty-six-year-old human could be to an orc except for...

Except for sex.

My chin wobbles at the terrifying thought. I'm to be a sex slave to some brutish orc, and judging by the size of these guys, it won't be a pleasant experience.

At least I'm not a virgin.

I push away the stray thought, trying to think of a way to escape. If I could just get away from them for a minute... But they'd even posted a full guard when I'd begged to attend to my bodily needs, like I was some sort of precious cargo.

And maybe I am. I narrow my eyes at the orc sitting beside me. If I'm valuable, maybe that's my bargaining chip.

Before I can go down that line of thought, the wagon slows, and noise erupts around us, many voices clamoring all at once. The horses whinny, and for a moment, fear shoots through me. If we're being attacked by bandits, I'll lose what little protection I have in my current situation.

It's sobering to realize that I now prefer the company of

these two orcs and their band of soldiers to other kinds of orcs. At least my current captors—owners—haven't sought to harm me.

Then the tone of the calls registers. They're happy greetings, even though the voices are gruff and deep.

More orcs, then.

Neekar brandishes a large hunting knife, and I cringe away from him, yelping in fear. But he rolls his eyes, grabs my tied wrists, and slashes the rope tying me. I struggle out of my restraints and rub my wrists, though in truth, the knots weren't tight enough to chafe my skin.

Then I lean forward and peer out the back of the covered wagon. I can't see much apart from the forest, but the crowd of orcs gathered to receive us is a glaring clue.

We have arrived.

CHAPTER
TWO

Ozork jumps out of the wagon, lowers a set of steps, and offers me a hand. I take it—I would much rather exit by myself but I don't trust my legs right now.

Not with the mass of strangely quiet orcs watching my every move.

"Come on," Ozork says. "Don't be afraid."

Easy for him to say.

He's as large, brutish, and green as the rest of them. Unlike me. I'm not a small woman, but every orc warrior I've met so far has towered over me, taller by a head or more. They could crush me with those big fists, break me with thick arms.

Ozork positions himself at my front, Neekar at my back, and we move through the crowd and deeper into the forest. Orcs part for us, but some of them linger, leaning in for a quick sniff of me. Neekar bats them back with sharp words of reprimand and keeps them from touching me.

At first, I don't understand what's so special about this part of the forest—why we stopped here or why all these orcs have gathered to wait for us in this exact spot.

The uneven ground is hard to walk on, moss-covered boulders dotting the forest floor. It would be quite beautiful and serene if it wasn't for the throng of shuffling, murmuring orcs following us.

Then I see it. A wooden hatch built into the side of a small rise, the wood camouflaged so well, it melds with the forest almost seamlessly. Only the faint glimmer of a black iron keyhole betrays it for what it is. An entrance to an orc dwelling.

Suddenly, similar doors appear all around us—or rather, I know what to look for now, so I see them clearly. More orcs peer from those openings. An orc woman stands with a baby on her hip, her face lit up in curiosity, and an elderly orc couple gaze at me with what I can only assume is hostility.

They've brought me to a forest settlement. And everywhere I look, more orcs are gawping at me. It's true, then. Every story I've heard. They're hulking, uncouth barbarians who live in holes in the ground.

I don't know why I'm surprised.

We continue upward until we reach a dip in the slope. I squint at it—in the twilight, it's hard to make out anything among the lichen-covered trees and rocks. Then the door swings outward, a massive, thick slab of oakwood reinforced with black iron. And in the opening stands a male with an iron crown on his head.

The orc king.

I didn't even know orcs had kingdoms. Or any sort of political structure apart from ruthless bands that pillage the human lands. But the deep bows of my guards—strong warriors both—and every orc who followed us in a procession to this place tell me they either respect or fear their ruler.

9

Silence descends on the forest, marred only by the occasional sniff from behind me. It's as if the gathered orcs are still trying to smell me.

The king steps forward. He's taller than Neekar and broader in the shoulders. Where Neekar is young for a warrior, the male in front of me has clearly seen battle and hardship—scars pepper his arms, and even though he's wearing a sleeveless linen tunic over his leather pants, he looks uncivilized.

"Welcome, warriors of the Black Bear Clan." His voice booms over the crowd. "Thank you for bringing back this woman and the provisions for our city."

Ah, so the other wagons in our guarded convoy must have been filled with purchases from Ultrup. Considering the fact that their settlement seems to be situated in the middle of the forest, I can't imagine they're a farming people. I wonder what they have to trade for the things they need. Furs, maybe?

"Tonight, we will feast," the king continues. "But first, let us see if our new guest might be matched with one of you."

His dark gaze lands on me, and I stiffen. What does he mean, *matched* with one of them?

The orcs roar in answer, though, their eyes all trained on me. Some are hopeful, some downright leering, but all are monstrous and horrible.

All my suspicions are coming true. They've brought me here to be a slave to one of these brutes.

I tense, wondering if I could outrun them. If I caused some sort of distraction and bolted for the deep forest, could I make it far enough for them to lose my trail?

No.

They're stronger, larger, and know the territory much

better than me. My poor choice of clothing and shoes would also be a hindrance, compared to the orcs' heavy boots.

There seems to be some sort of order to what's happening around me. The male orcs—and several women —form two lines facing each other. They create a corridor with roughly four feet of space between them, extending from me toward the king.

Neekar gives me a gentle push from behind. "Go on."

I peer up at him. "Why? What will they do?"

"Nothing. Unless one of them is your mate," he mutters. "It is a great honor to become mated."

"Great honor for whom?" I squeak.

But all the orcs are staring at me expectantly, and I know I only have two options. I can either walk down the double line on my own or someone will carry me.

I step forward, putting one foot in front of the other. The first pair of orcs, one on either side of me, lean in and inhale deeply. I can't imagine the experience is pleasant, what with my dirty gown and unwashed body, but no one is forcing them to do it.

I lift my head higher. They could at least have had the decency to allow me to bathe. But no, they wanted to do this straight away. Serves them right if they get a good whiff of my sweat.

Slowly, I advance down the line. No one touches me, and with every pair of orcs I pass, my hope grows a little stronger.

Maybe I won't get matched with anyone.

If that happens, maybe they'll let me go. Or maybe they'll chain me up somewhere and force me to be their slave anyway, for all I know. But at least I won't have to endure being bound to one of these creatures.

With that thought in mind, I quicken my steps, almost tripping in my hurry. Orcs around me grunt with displeasure, taking quick, hasty sniffs of me, but I don't care. If I can make it to the end of the line, I'll be free.

The orc king grows larger the closer I get to him. He's waiting in front of the door, arms crossed, an almost bored expression on his rough-hewn face. No matter the speech he gave his people, their ruler doesn't think much of me—or the idea of being matched. He doesn't put himself in the line, doesn't lean forward eagerly to catch my scent.

So I keep my gaze on him. If I can make it to him...

The last pair of orcs step in, inhaling. They're large warriors, with weapons belts bristling with steel. But neither of them seems affected. They retreat, their faces reflecting twin expressions of disappointment before they mask it quickly. So they want this—they want *me*. Whatever this mating thing is, it's desirable enough for them to show emotion.

Mere steps separate me from the orc king now. I slow down, panicked breaths quieting. I've made it. I walked through the crowd, and no one claimed me, so I'll—

The king's nostrils flare.

My belly tightens at the fierce expression on his face. But not in fear—no, this isn't the response I'm used to. *What...?*

He lurches forward, then stops himself as if the movement was involuntary. He inhales deeply through his nose, and a loud growl reverberates from his chest.

"Mine."

THREE

My feet won't move. No matter how hard I try to tell myself to pick up my skirts and *run*, my body won't obey me. I'm frozen in place, pinned to the spot by the intensity of the king's stare.

His black eyes widened with shock a moment earlier, but right now, he's glowering at me, eyes narrowed in suspicion.

As if I'm the problem.

As if I willingly came here and foisted myself upon him.

Since I can't escape, I do the next best thing. I throw back my shoulders and glower.

He steps closer, angling his head to the side. Even from a distance, I guessed he was tall, but the reality of just how much taller he is than me hits me when I'm suddenly face-to-face with the laces of his tunic.

I refuse to crane my neck to look up at him. If he wants to speak to me, he should—

His big, green-skinned hand comes up to my face. He grips my chin, the hold gentle but firm, and tilts my face up.

"Hello, little mate."

His voice is meant for me only, and it doesn't carry. It's a rough caress against my sensitive nerves, and I bristle.

I draw in an outraged breath, ready to chew him out.

And I stop. Because the most delicious scent washes over me, an aroma so inviting and powerful, I sway on my feet. It reminds me of deep forests, washed by spring rains, of crackling fires and safety.

I want to wrap myself in it and forget about all my troubles.

It's *him*.

The orc king smells like home.

I jerk away from him, slapping a hand over my nose and mouth.

"What are you doing?" I gasp past my fingers. "Stop it."

The orc squares his shoulders, and a coldness descends on his handsome features. In a blink, he's next to me. He drapes one strong arm around my shoulders and tucks me against his side. Then he turns us both to face the waiting crowd.

"Tonight, we celebrate. I have found my queen."

Cheers erupt in the silent forest. Orcs crowd around us, pressing in, slapping the king's shoulders and shaking my hand. A young orc woman with tears in her eyes even wraps me in a bone-crushing hug and pats my cheek as if I'm everything she's been hoping for. I cringe back more and more, overwhelmed, until the king squeezes me more firmly and holds me away from the pressing throng.

He peers down at me. "Are you all right?"

I can only stare at him, wide-eyed. He grumbles something unintelligible under his breath, and suddenly I'm being escorted through the door, into the Hill. A tall entrance chamber narrows to a hallway barely wide

14

enough for us to walk side by side. Given how the king glared at me earlier, I thought he was going to dismiss me once we weren't surrounded by his people anymore, but he keeps his arm around my shoulders and leads me deeper into the underground dwelling.

Corridors branch out on both sides, and doorways lead to chambers big and small, and soon, I get lost trying to count the twists and turns we take. The Hill must be completely hollowed out, and what I thought was a simple burrow seems to be a complex warren, an anthill of epic proportions.

"Where are you taking me?" I manage to force out.

He pulls me forward, and I stumble in the dimming light, tripping over some stone or tree root or whatever litters these musty corridors. No lanterns light the way, and I realize the orcs must have better eyesight than humans because soon, I can no longer see anything past the faintest outlines.

The king stops, and I think he's about to answer me, but he clicks his tongue impatiently, the sound so human it confuses me. Then he swoops down, hooks one arm beneath my knees, and picks me up as if I weigh nothing. Wordlessly, he strides forward, and now that I don't have to watch my feet, I sense two guards following close behind us.

"Let me go," I demand.

He doesn't listen. Of course not. He's the orc king, and I'm the woman his warriors bought at the slave market.

At last, we stop at another door, not too different from the one at the entrance to the underground village. The guards silently take their places, one on each side of the door, and neither look at me.

They probably know what's going to happen to me now.

The king has found his mate, and he intends to take me.

I struggle in his arms, pushing against his broad chest to get him to release me, but he's much too strong. All the while, the insidious scent of his skin invades my senses, driving me out of my mind. One of the guards throws open the door, and I curse at him. He *knows* what the king will do to me, and yet he stands there, staring at the wall like nothing is going on.

"Savages!" I shriek. "You'll all pay for this!"

The king kicks the door shut behind us and dumps me unceremoniously on the bed. I scramble away from him and fall over the edge on the other side. My ass lands on something soft—the floor of the king's bedroom is lined with furs.

Luxurious, silky pelts of some long-haired beast that the orcs apparently hunt for. I dig my fingers in on reflex. I've never felt anything like it before. In my previous life, such extravagant items were only meant for nobility.

But that's not important right now. I need to get away, which means I need to find a weapon to defend myself. He may have bought me, but I'm no slave. And I'm not going down without a fight. I cast around for anything I can use, anything at all. A knife, a stick, or maybe scissors? Something sharp to poke him with.

But the king isn't moving. He stands on the other side of the bed, his big fists on his hips. The white tusks jutting from his lower lip would have shocked me if I hadn't spent the past week in the company of the other orcs. But this male is taller than all of the warriors I've met so far, his muscles bunching beneath his sleeveless linen tunic. His green skin looks darker in the lamplight, as do his glittering eyes. But what throws me the most is his expression. He's watching me with a strange mixture of hopelessness and exasperation on his face.

I still. If he was going to attack me, he'd do it straight away, yes? Or would he wait for me to tire myself out? Maybe he just wants prey that struggles less.

Not wanting to wait for his decision, I stand and sidle over to the writing desk in the corner. For a moment, it strikes me as incongruous that the orc king has a writing desk, littered with quills and papers. I had no idea orcs were even literate. The stories that circulate through the taverns in the human towns certainly never mentioned anything like it. Then my gaze snags on the small knife lying on top of a stack of notes, probably used for sharpening the quills.

If I could but grab it, I might have a chance of making it out of here. The blade is short, but it doesn't need to be long for me to stick it into his neck. Orcs might be bigger and stronger than humans, but they're similar enough. If struck correctly, he would bleed just the same.

I prepare myself to lunge for it...

"Don't."

The king's voice snaps out, rough and deep. I freeze, my hand extended to the side. All right, so he saw through my intentions. I'll have to be faster. With all that bulk, he can't be—

He lunges forward, quick as a snake, and snatches the blade from his desk. Then he throws the knife across the room. A loud smack, and the blade embeds itself into the closed door, vibrating with the power of the impact.

I gape at it, all my will to fight draining from me. The king's message is loud and clear. He's a killing machine, and if he wanted to, that knife could easily be sticking from my ribs right now.

My hands tremble, and I grip them together behind my back, refusing to let him know he has gotten to me. The movement pushes my breasts out to strain against my dress, and his gaze drops to my cleavage, so I quickly release my hands and draw back from the king, a fresh spike of fear lancing my heart.

The king reaches for his crown, places it on the desk, and rubs his forehead. "I don't want to hurt you."

I have only one answer to this. "Then let me go."

He looks up, expression almost rueful. "I cannot."

"Why?" I ask, proud that my voice doesn't crack. "Why would you want to keep me?"

"Because you're my mate." His face turns grim, and he paces away from me. "For better or for worse, the gods chose you for me. I will do what I must."

I throw my hands up. "Thank you. I'm sure this will be a comfort to me when you force yourself on me."

He swivels around, glowering at me. The force of his anger has me retreating a step.

The big male stalks forward, and his voice vibrates with fury. "I would not do that. I told you I don't want to hurt you."

"And I should take you at your word?" I cry. "Your men *bought* me. Imprisoned me. And dragged me halfway across the continent to this hovel. So forgive me if I'm not in a trusting mood."

"You mock my home and yet you come here smelling like you've been rolling in a ditch," he sneers at me.

My cheeks heat. "It's your guards who forced me to sleep on the ground like some animal."

"And they didn't give you a chance to clean yourself?" he demands.

I scoff. "In a river, yes. While they all watched me."

He raises his eyebrows, as if to say, *Yes, and?*

"I couldn't undress to wash properly," I growl, frustration rising inside me. "I haven't had a chance to change or clean my gown in more than a week. And before that, I was kept in the slave barracks, where they barely gave us water to drink, let alone wash ourselves."

The orc king lets out a defeated sigh. "I forget how prudish humans are."

"Prudish?" I straighten my shoulders, ready to defend my kin. "I'm not prudish."

"An orc would rather go naked than wear clothes as dirty as yours," he retorts. "Yet you insist on covering your body with filthy scraps in the name of propriety. Tell me, which is more shameful?"

And somehow, this orc—this clean, well-dressed, amazing-smelling orc—questioning my propriety, accusing me of shameful behavior, is too much for me. My throat tightens, and the tremor from my hands spreads all over my body. Suddenly, I can't hold it back anymore—the tears, the fear, the overwhelming certainty that this is where my life will end.

I sniffle and hold the king's gaze because I'm damned if I will look away. I also don't want to turn my back on him, because no matter what he says about not hurting me, I don't trust him. I can't afford to. Whenever I've trusted anyone in my life, they stabbed me in the back. Beginning with my parents.

The king makes a low sound in his throat and closes the distance between us. "Don't cry, little mate."

He brings his hand up and swipes his thumb over my cheek. I blink hard and try to hold back the tears, but they overflow anyway. And once I start, I can't seem to stop.

"No," he says, almost angry now. "No crying."

He takes my shoulders in a grip and gives me a light squeeze.

"I-I'm sorry," I choke out and smack my hand on his chest. It's ridiculously firm—and so, so warm. "This is what humans do when we're upset."

He stares down at me for a long moment. Then he wraps his arms around me and squashes me close. I yelp and stumble forward, and suddenly, I'm surrounded by muscle and warm, green skin. The cool linen of his tunic scratches against my cheek, but my mind zeroes in on one sensation only.

The rapid, steady beat of his heart.

The king might present a hard exterior, but he must feel something underneath it all. For me.

The comforting, clean scent of him invades my senses with every breath, and I let myself lean into it for just a minute. Maybe it makes me horribly naïve, but in that instant, I can almost, *almost* believe his words.

"What is your name?" he asks quietly.

With my cheek pressed to his chest, I feel the sound of his voice more than hear it. The sensation is not unpleasant. I've never experienced it before, which strikes me as unbearably sad. Instead of bursting into tears again, I focus on his question.

I could lie. The orc guards who bought me at auction didn't press when I refused to tell them, and I'd thought that maybe my name wasn't important if I was going to remain a slave. But the king says I'm his mate. Surely, he genuinely wants to know?

"What's yours?" I counter.

I'm not giving away anything for free. If I've learned anything in all the years I've been taking care of myself, it's that everything has a price. And if he wants my name, he'll have to work for it, too.

He loosens his hold and looks down at me. A slight smile curves his lips, the white tusks gleaming. "It's Gorvor, son of Trak."

"Gorvor," I repeat, savoring the name. It suits him. "I'm Dawn."

His grip on my waist tightens. "Beautiful."

Heat rises in my cheeks. I don't know if he means me or the name, but the way he says it is so sincere, something fragile blooms in the deepest, most secret corner of my heart.

Stupid.

The angry voice in my head has me lowering my gaze and stomping down on any tender feelings. I have no business allowing this orc to get past my defenses.

He stiffens and lets go of me. His warmth disappears when he steps back and clears his throat. "You should change your dress. There's no time for a bath, but you'll find a basin and a washcloth over there."

I squint at the other side of the underground room. Between my conviction that he brought me here to take advantage of me and my breakdown, I didn't even notice the recessed area of the king's bedchamber. But there's a large pool of water, maybe six feet across, by the far wall.

"How is this possible?" I step forward, intrigued in spite of everything. "Did you have servants fill it?"

Behind me, the king's footsteps are nearly silent on the clean-swept clay floor. "There's a thermal spring inside the Hill," he says. "That's why this settlement was built here. It holds many surprises."

I crouch by the edge of the water and dip my hand in it. "It's warm!"

A huff of breath that could almost count as a laugh has me looking up. The king—Gorvor—stands so close to me. He could easily tip me over into the pool, and I'm a little surprised he hasn't already, for all his insistence that I should clean myself.

"So you...bathe here?" I ask.

"Aye," he says. "And so will you. Once we get through the celebration."

Ah. At that, I stand again. "You keep mentioning the celebration. What's going on?"

He spreads his arms a little. "The king has found his mate. His queen. My people will want to feast."

The words echo in my mind for a long, silent moment. *His mate. His queen.*

"You mean me?" I gape at him. "A queen?"

He clicks his tongue, and I get the sense that he's annoyed at how slow I'm being. But it's not every day a woman gets presented to a clan full of orcs, only to be dragged to their king's chamber. I've been through a *lot* this week, and I don't appreciate his attitude at all.

"You're telling me you want me to stand in front of your people and become your *queen* a mere hour after I arrived?" My voice rises with each word, but I don't care. "I won't be paraded around. I won't! I want food and a chance to rest."

I stomp my foot to underscore my point, feeling like a petulant child. This has gone far enough, though. But Gorvor crosses his big arms over his chest and stares at me until I dip my gaze to the ground.

Then he speaks in a low, harsh rumble. "My people expect to see their queen at the feast. You will clean your-self up and put on fresh clothes. There will be food at the celebration. But you will smile and you will behave like you're perfectly happy to be there, or you will see a very different side of me. Do you understand?"

I jerk my chin down because what else can I do? He has finally shown his colors, threatening me with swift retribution should I disobey him. I wonder what he means to achieve by having me pretend I'm happy, though. Surely, if his people kidnap and buy women to find mates, they are used to them kicking and screaming? But maybe it's a pride thing. Maybe he wants his people to believe I'm completely smitten with him.

"What am I expected to do?" I ask. "I don't know how an orc bride is supposed to behave."

"You will eat and drink and you will not be rude to my people or my guests." He leans in, meeting my gaze. "And you will sit in my lap. All night."

Up until that last order, I didn't think him too demanding. But to sit in his lap all night...

"If you want me to do all that, I want something in return," I blurt out.

He narrows his eyes at me but motions at me to speak.

"I want you to promise that you won't touch me tonight."

He draws back, outraged. "Impossible. Orcs touch each other all the time. And I just said you will be—"

"All right, I meant to say that you won't, you know, force me to do anything *else* tonight."

I probably shouldn't interrupt the king, but damn propriety. I have none of it left in any case.

"I told you I wouldn't," he growls.

"Your word, sir," I demand.

He stares down at me, fuming. But finally, he offers me his hand. "I give you my word."

We shake hands, and for some reason, I believe him.

FOUR

The next half hour passes in a flurry of preparations. Just as I'm about to ask for a fresh gown, a knock on the door announces the young orc woman who hugged me earlier. She shoves an armful of velvet, linen, and silk at Gorvor through the crack in the door. Her curious gaze lands on me for a brief second, and she beams, showing off white teeth. Then the king slams the door in her face. Before I can berate him for his rudeness, he tells me the woman is his nosy cousin who has been pestering him to find a mate for ages.

It's such a normal tidbit that I almost slip and forget that I'm no longer in the human kingdom, but the tall orc immediately reminds me where I am by refusing to set up a privacy screen for me. He says they don't even exist in his Hill, and that I should get used to the orc ways.

Still, I manage to convince him to turn his back on me while I strip off the filthy gown and chemise and scrub myself with a soft washcloth and a fresh-smelling chunk of good, creamy soap. My hair is a mess, but since he won't give me the time to bathe, I can only run a comb through it and braid it tight, hoping no one will come close enough to see how greasy it really is.

"Are you ready?" the king grumbles from where he's sitting at his desk, hunched over some correspondence. "We need to go."

I tie the ribbons of my chemise and struggle into a plum-colored velvet gown that Gorvor picked for me. While it's well crafted and has a little black bear embroidered at the neckline, it's loose around my bosom and tight around my hips, so the woman it was made for clearly had a better figure than me. But I don't suppose the orcs will care.

"I need help with the laces," I admit. "I think this belonged to a lady with handmaidens at some point."

Gorvor shifts in his chair, his dark gaze unreadable. "It belonged to no one. Our seamstresses make clothes in advance so we can give them to humans who arrive to our lands. Most come with no possessions, so we are always prepared."

I stare at him, trying to comprehend what he's saying. This means they have a steady influx of kidnapped, bought women, doesn't it? Right when I think he might be a decent person, he goes on and tells me something like this.

"How nice of you," I say dryly.

If he catches my tone, he doesn't show it. He stands, once more dwarfing me with his height, and walks closer. He takes me by my shoulders and turns me around, the warmth of his palms seeping through the fabric of my dress.

"Tighten the laces," I murmur. "Please."

He grumbles, "I don't know if my hands were made for this."

No, I don't imagine they were.

"Just do your best," I say.

25

He tugs, and one of the laces snaps. Gorvor growls in frustration, then ties the rest with care, slowly moving up my back.

"I will get you a better gown." His warm breath brushes the back of my neck. "If you can't even dress yourself, what's the point of wearing clothing?"

"That's something ladies everywhere have been asking for ages," I quip.

He lets out another one of those huffs, and for the first time since I arrived, I feel a certain kind of kinship with this orc. There's no telling what will happen to me here, but at least the king knows how to laugh.

"Come," he says finally and picks up his crown, setting it back on his head. "We are late."

Apprehension slams into me again. "Wait! Will more orcs try to sniff me?"

I smell marginally better now, but I don't relish the thought of being put on display again. Of being smelled and crowded and leered at.

"No," he answers, his black eyebrows snapping down. "You are mine. No one else's. No one would dare."

"Oh." I brush back a stray lock of my hair. "All right, then. I'm ready."

He opens the door for me, and the two guards stationed outside straighten their shoulders. I glare at both of them—neither one of them helped me when I'd screamed earlier. They likely knew that their king wouldn't hurt me, but I didn't know that. They could have taken the time to at least reassure me.

My dirty glares don't seem to bother them in the slightest, though. One of them stares ahead, his expression blank, but the other gives me a grin and winks, his black eyes twinkling with amusement.

26

"These are Steagor and Vark," the king announces, pointing to the two warriors in turn. "When I cannot be with you, they will be your guards."

That has me standing straight. "What? Why would I need guards?"

Gorvor wraps his massive arm around my shoulders and tugs me along the dark corridor. "You are my queen. Of course you need guards. You are now my greatest vulnerability."

He says the words without inflection, and I don't know what to think. He's admitting to having a weakness—in front of his men, even. This must mean he trusts them completely. Or maybe this is common knowledge.

I try to follow along with him as best I can, clinging on to him for support so I don't stumble. "You mean because I'm a weak human?"

He snorts. "Aye. And because you won't let me touch you."

I want to ask what he's talking about, but a snatch of music drifts down the corridor, and Gorvor snaps to attention. His entire demeanor changes, and he pulls me in tight against his side.

"Remember. Happy."

He glares down at me, and I realize I can make out his expression because the corridor has grown steadily lighter. We round a bend in the corridor, and a large opening yawns in front of us, filled with the flickering glow of torchlight. At the threshold of the open space, the king stops.

And I can only stare. We've come to what must be the main hall of the settlement, deep underground. The chamber is massive, filled with rows of tables and benches, and at the far end, a large carved wooden chair stands behind a table laid with a feast fit for royalty. It's a

27

dining space and a throne room combined, and everywhere I look, orcs are milling around, clearly waiting for something.

It takes them a moment to notice us, but when they do, a hush falls over the crowd.

The king's grip on me tightens, and he raises his hand in a salute.

Orc men and women, too many to count, raise their fists in the air and holler greetings, congratulations, and well-wishes for the king and his bride. For *me*. The noise is overpowering, and I flinch, doing my best to keep my hands at my sides, even though I'd like nothing more than to clap them over my ears.

"Come," Gorvor says, tugging me forward.

We make our way between the tables, and the king accepts pats on the back and cheerful ribbing about how he's the lucky one tonight. He returns every smile and compliment, and I could almost believe he's genuinely happy to have me by his side, if he hadn't admitted to me earlier that he sees me as a vulnerability.

Finally, we reach the cloth-covered table with the throne, and the king motions at someone, a signal that has the kitchen staff carrying out platters the size of shields, heaped with roasted meat and bread, cauldrons of stew, and baskets of ripe late-summer fruit. The crowd of orcs murmur appreciatively as they sit, and the feast begins.

Gorvor settles himself on the throne. It's sturdy and wide, a beautifully carved piece of oiled oakwood with the grain of the wood visible. Whoever made it must have been a skilled craftsman. Its legs look like bear paws, and on the high back is an image of a roaring bear's face, its fearsome teeth whittled in perfect detail. The chair is large enough to hold the king without seeming cramped, which means it would be entirely too big for me. Not that I would want to sit on the throne of this orc kingdom.

But Gorvor apparently hasn't forgotten what he told me in his bedroom. With one quick move, he scoops me off the floor and settles me in his lap. The gathered orcs cheer at the move, raising their cups to us.

I desperately fight a blush, hoping the flickering torchlight might hide it from the king. "Is this really necessary?"

His warm hand lands on my belly, and he pulls me up his chest. "Aye. Now stop squirming."

The low vibration of his voice still has that strange effect on me. My muscles soften, and I relax slightly, leaning back. He's just so *warm*, and in the crowded hall, he's my only anchor.

"Are you hungry?" he asks.

"Yes."

I lean forward to reach for a plate and cutlery, but Gorvor's arm restricts my movements.

"I will do this for you," he announces.

Craning my neck to look at him, I stare at his serious profile. His jaw is clenched tight, and when I shift my weight again to give him more room, he stills, wincing.

That's when I realize that what I thought was one of the muscles in his massive thigh is actually...

"Oh!" Heat rushes through me, and I berate myself for being so silly. A panicked part of my mind is stuck thinking about how *big* the king's cock is, how hard and hot under my ass, while the curious side of me wonders at how it would even work. I nip that thought in the bud and force it deep, deep down.

"Woman," Gorvor forces out through gritted teeth. "You need to stay still."

"All right," I breathe. "I'm sorry."

29

He slants his gaze at me, and the corner of his mouth tips up in a grim smile. "Took you long enough to notice."

I reach for his arm and give him a hard pinch. "Don't be a beast."

His eyes darken, and he leans in, running his nose up the side of my neck. He inhales deeply. "But that's what I am."

Swallowing thickly, I stay frozen, so much like prey. Yes, he is a beast, and I would be wise to remember it. But it's difficult to keep my thoughts focused on that when he smells so good. When he clearly wants me.

He would be just as hard and ready for any other woman if he thought she was his mate.

The reminder serves as a mental bucket of cold water, bringing me back to my senses. Then my stomach growls with hunger, and the king snaps to attention once more.

"Forgive me," he says. "I didn't mean to keep you waiting."

He fills a plate for me, adding a hunk of dark bread, a good cut of juicy meat, and a ripe pear he swiftly quarters with a hunting knife he pulls from his belt. The way he offers me food makes me think it might be some sort of ritual, and he keeps his gaze on me until I take my first bite of the still-warm bread.

It's good fare, simple but well prepared, and I compliment the cook's skill. One of the two guards, who had stationed themselves behind the throne, moves to the side to pass my words on to a servant, and moments later, a bright-eyed man appears in front of our table, bringing us an assortment of sweet rolls and custards.

He disappears again before I can do anything more than thank him, and Gorvor chuckles at the exchange.

"You did good, little mate," he rumbles.

I raise my eyebrows. "What did I do?"

"You got on the cook's good side," he says. "That's always a smart thing to do."

I try one of everything from the platter of sweets, then offer them to Steagor and Vark, who glance at the king for permission before digging in and demolishing the delicacies.

Gorvor rubs his thumb up and down my belly, a small movement that somehow becomes the center of my attention.

"You offered them food," he murmurs in my ear. "I was worried you were going to have to work for their loyalty, but now I think they will gladly defend you with their lives."

I snort, pleased that I apparently got something else right this evening. "Should I have offered you a pastry, then?"

His grip on me tightens, and he spreads his thighs slightly, letting me feel the length of his thick cock. "I'm already yours."

The words shouldn't mean anything to me. But in my old life, I'd never belonged. Not with my family, not in my village, and certainly not in the bed of the man who took my innocence in exchange for a couple of silver coins. Here, though, the orcs seem genuinely pleased with the fact that I'm their king's mate.

And the king himself... Well, I'm not sure he's pleased with his human bride, but I can't deny that he wants me.

He pours a cup of pale-yellow liquid in a silver cup and hands it to me. "It's time for the toasts."

I look at him in question, but he shakes his head and pours himself a drink, too.

"Take small sips," he warns me. "This will take a while."

And he is right. One by one, various orcs, both men and women, stand from their benches and wish us well.

"...and may your queen bear you many strong children," concludes a particularly long-winded, elderly orc who salutes us with his cup.

The crowd cheers, and everyone takes a swallow of their drink. The children in the crowd yell the loudest, apparently happy to make noise, though none of them have been allowed to have what we're drinking. I bring my cup to my lips once more and pretend to take a sip of the delicious—but strong—mead. My head is pleasantly fuzzy, and I no longer mind that Gorvor is holding me so close to his chest. In fact, I suspect his big arm is the only thing keeping me upright at the moment.

Then I get distracted by the thick cords of muscle in his upper arm. I squeeze the bulge that's as big as my head and let out a sigh. He's so strong.

Vark snickers beside the throne, and I realize I must have said that out loud.

"Forgive me," I demur, peering up at the king through my eyelashes.

He grimaces like he's in pain, but he doesn't admonish me. "I should have watered down your mead. I didn't realize you might not be used to it at all."

I shrug. "When you don't have money for food, buying alcohol doesn't make sense."

The king's gaze darkens, and I smack my hand over my mouth. *Oops.* I didn't mean to say *that* out loud, either. For some reason, I don't want Gorvor to know how shitty my life was before I was kidnapped and dragged to that auction house. Maybe it's pride. Or self-preservation. If I can pretend that everything was fine, then I don't have to think about the things I'd had to do to survive.

He looks like he might say something, but a loud scraping of a bench across the clay floor catches my attention.

Four orcs stand as one, their faces grim. Before, each of the well-wishers had a little speech of their own, but these four seem united. There's something different about them, and I squint, trying to figure it out. Then it hits me—the emblem at the front of their tunics is different from those I've seen on the other guests. Gorvor and most of his people carry a small image of a roaring bear sewn into their clothes, the same as the one on my dress, and the image is repeated in the carved decorations in the room, as well as the flags by the entrance to the underground cavern.

But these four orcs show off a different image. It's hard to make out from a distance, but I think it must be a boar— that, or a rabbit, and I cannot imagine that these soldiers would willingly pick a bunny as their symbol.

The second orc from the left raises his cup and speaks. "Congratulations to the king and his new queen. May you find safety and happiness in each other's arms. We hope your reign will be a long and fruitful one."

The rest of the orcs lift their cups and cheer, but I'm either growing very tired and drunk, or the exclamations have grown rather half-hearted. I glance up at Gorvor to find him gritting his teeth, but he salutes the orcs none-theless and takes a sip of his drink. I imitate him, not wanting to offend anyone, but I don't understand the sudden tension in the room.

The four orcs take their places again, and the murmur of the conversation rises once more to a roar as the rest of Gorvor's clansmen go back to drinking, eating, and laugh-ing. Someone produces a fiddle, and several orcs take up a loud, bawdy song. More join them for the refrain, and the hall echoes with laughter. A child falls asleep at the table, and his father picks him up and carries him off into a corridor on the other side of the hall.

"Time to go," Gorvor mutters a while later. "They will continue for hours, but I think you've had enough for tonight, hmm?"

I blink up at him, confused. At some point, I stopped caring about what others would think of me, and now my cheek is pressed against the king's warm chest, and I'm half asleep, tired and more than a little drunk.

"All right," I manage to say. "But I don't know the way back."

Gorvor gives me a small, private smile. "Don't worry. I won't let you get lost."

The next thing I know, he has me in his arms, carrying me through the hall. Orcs cheer and wave at us, calling out suggestions about our first mating night that have my cheeks burning with embarrassment. Gorvor takes it all in stride, though, and tightens his grip on me when I squirm.

"Your people have no shame," I complain once we enter the dark corridor, the two guards trailing behind us. "What happens between a man and a woman is their own business."

The king hums. "Maybe in the human world. Here, things are different. You will do well to let go of what you have learned."

Tired as I am, I refuse to be patronized. "No, thank you."

The king is silent for a moment, and the darkness closes around us. I remember that we're underground, and the thought of all the earth around us is a little terrifying, though strangely, the air isn't stuffy.

"You know what would be nice?" I blurt, hating the

silence between us. "If there was more light in these corridors."

Gorvor's answer comes slowly, as if he's lost in thought. "Then I would have no excuse to carry you."

I can't help it—the words melt another bit of the icy wall I've put up inside me. He's so honest about wanting me, I can't fault him for it. Then he stops in the pitch darkness, and a door swings open.

We've returned to his bedroom.

This time, I don't scream at the guards who remain stationed outside. A brief thought passes through my fuzzy brain that it's strange that the guards are needed *inside* the Hill, but I'm too tired to give it much attention.

Instead, I let the king carry me over the threshold. He sets me on the bed, then returns to the door and bolts it from the inside and turns a large iron key in the lock. He pauses with his back to me and lets out a long breath.

His shoulders lower, and it hits me at that moment that he's been tense ever since we left his chamber to attend the dinner. Only now, in the privacy of his room, he seems to let go of whatever worried him.

That he trusts me enough to relax in my presence is humbling. Is his belief that I'm his true mate that strong? He only met me today, so I don't know what to think about that. Or maybe he finds me so insignificant, he doesn't care that he's showing me his true self.

That is much more likely. And disheartening.

"I'm tired," I begin, trying to keep my voice level. "I'd like to go to bed, please."

Gorvor gives me a small smile and shakes his head. "If you go to sleep now, you'll have a beast of a headache in the morning. Come, let's have a bath, and you can sober up first."

It's late, and my day has been so, so long. But I haven't had a proper bath in weeks. Not a warm one, anyway. At the inn where I worked before my kidnapping, I'd been the one to heat the water for the guests who requested a bath, so I never had the energy to carry bucket after bucket required to wash myself in comfort at home.

"Oh, fine," I grumble. "But I should likely drink some water, too."

Gorvor wordlessly walks over to where a pitcher and two cups stand by his bed and pours me a cup full of cool, clear water. His gaze remains on me, and I swallow the last of my drink, self-conscious because of his scrutiny.

Now I'll see if the king's word is worth anything—he's been drinking as much as me or more, even, and if he means to maul me, this is when he will do it.

But he just motions at me to move toward the bathing pool. "Go on."

I bite my lip, torn between wanting that bath and propriety. But the light vapors rising from the water make the decision for me. I imagine how good it will feel to sink to my neck, and the thought is too good to resist.

"Help me with my laces?" I turn my back to Gorvor.

He's more careful of the delicate ribbons this time, and he plucks one after another, loosening my dress.

"Thank you—" I begin to say, then stop.

Because he puts his fingers to my hair and starts pulling out the pins I'd used to hold my braids up. The light tugs aren't painful, but they make me aware of his looming presence behind me. I stand very still, clutching my dress to my chest while he unravels my braid and sifts his fingers through my hair.

He's being so gentle with me. My chest aches with the tenderness. When was the last time someone took their time to care for me? Even as we exited the great hall, he could have left me at my own mercy or demanded that one of his guards carry me. But he did all of it himself, as if it matters to him. As if *I* matter.

I swallow past a suddenly tight throat. "Thank you."

He strokes the backs of his fingers down my neck, the movement slow and sensual. "Get in the water."

The words are a clear command, but for once, I don't chafe against it. I glance over my shoulder, and he huffs in annoyance, then closes his eyes, giving me the tiniest bit of privacy. Quickly, I drop my dress, letting it slither from me, and untie the ribbons of my shift. Then I hurry to the edge of the pool, crouch next to it, and sit on the lip.

The moment my feet disappear beneath the water, I know this will be my favorite place in the settlement. Careful not to splash water everywhere, I lower myself into what is essentially a giant bathtub.

"Ohh."

A low sigh escapes me as the warmth closes around me like a gentle embrace. The water is exactly the right temperature, as warm as I can bear, and the knowledge that it won't turn cold even if I soak in here for hours seems like the greatest luxury. Better even than having servants heat up buckets of water over the fire. Anytime I want, I can dip in here without having to ask anyone.

I sink to my neck and make sure nothing scandalous is visible above the surface. I could float here forever, with my feet barely skimming the bottom. Feeling along the edge of the pool, I locate a carved ledge and settle on it, finally relaxed after a long, confusing day.

A rustle of clothing snags my attention. I glance up to find Gorvor stripping his linen tunic. The muscles of his abdomen and chest ripple with the movement, his green skin stretching. He drapes the tunic over his writing chair and faces me, then pauses.

I'm aware that I'm staring. But I can't look away.

His body is a work of art. Every chiseled contour, every dip and swell of his broad shoulders...he is *magnificent*. But large. He could snap me in two and not even breathe hard.

At last, I drag my gaze up from his chest to his face, only to find him grinning at me. That smile turns his harsh features into something I could consider handsome, if it wasn't for his tusks. But even those add a certain roguish charm to his face. Maybe it's the mead I drank, or maybe I'm turning soft in the head, but I flush under the power of his knowing gaze.

Then he puts his hands to the waistband of his leather pants, and I jerk to attention.

"What are you doing?" I demand, panicking.

He unties the laces slowly. "Taking a bath."

I should be looking at his face, but it's impossible. "At the same time as me?"

My voice comes out breathy, too high. Surely he doesn't mean to join me in here?

But Gorvor hooks his thumbs in his pants—and I squeak, turning away with a splash of water. He doesn't answer me, but he doesn't have to. Of course he's taking a bath with me. Orcs have no sense of propriety, and he is the king of them all.

The water ripples as he lowers his big body into the pool behind me.

Then his order comes in a voice that's deeper than before.

"Turn around, little mate."

FIVE

I stand rooted to the spot, unwilling to face the orc behind me. Is this the moment he goes back on his word and ravishes me?

His deep sigh is the only warning before his hands take my shoulders. He turns me, still keeping hold of me, and stares down into my eyes.

"I will not hurt you," he says, and the words have the power of an oath.

They're low and sincere, spoken just for me, and gods help me, I believe him.

"All right," I whisper.

He lets go, floats back a pace, and reaches for a cake of soap. "Here. Wash yourself."

Right. Because I still smell, despite that hasty clean-up from before. Blushing, I take the soap from him and lather my hands, then sit on the ledge to methodically wash every limb. Gorvor does the same on his side of the pool. He dips his head underwater and washes his long black hair, then disappears beneath the surface again to rinse himself off. In the low candlelight, his body turns into a sculpted work of art, water sluicing down his powerful arms.

I take a deep breath and dive under, raking my fingers through my hair to thoroughly wet it. When I surface, Gorvor is watching me intently.

"I want to wash your hair," he says.

It's not really a question, nor is it a plea, and yet he waits for my answer. It's that hesitation on his part that convinces me to allow it. Big as he is, he could have easily overpowered me and taken whatever he wishes, but even though he has no sense of privacy, he is curbing his will to make me feel safe.

So I give him a small nod and face away from him. Gentle waves lap at my skin as he steps closer. He takes the soap from me, and the rhythmic slide and squelch tells me he's rubbing it between his palms. He soaps up the crown of my head first, then works the lather into my hair, rubbing my scalp with strong fingers. He moves this way and that, making sure he doesn't miss anything, and the look of concentration on his serious face has me stifling an unexpected smile.

It feels good. The last person to wash my hair had been my mother, and almost two decades have passed since then. She was never a loving parent, and I'd had to learn to take care of myself quite young. But tonight, I don't want to think about her.

Not when my orc mate is doing his best to lull me into a stupor with his skilled hands.

"Is this enough?" he asks, his voice gruff.

"Yes." I press my palm to the center of his chest for a brief second. "Thank you."

Before he can say anything more or touch me again, I dip my head under, washing away the suds. When I resurface, I find Gorvor has retreated to the other side of the pool and is relaxed against the edge, his head tipped back, his black gaze on me.

I bite my lip, unsure of how to say what I need to say. Then I decide to go for the truth, because orcs don't seem to be scandalized by anything.

"I want you to turn around," I say, raising my chin a little. "I need to wash my private parts."

The king smirks at me. "No."

"What do you mean, no?" I splutter.

"No."

He moves one hand from where it was leaning on the edge of the pool and dips it in the water. I can't see exactly what he's doing, but given what I just said to him, I can definitely imagine.

"Oh gods, will you stop?" I slap a hand over my eyes and retreat until the ledge pokes me in the backs of my thighs. Then I peer through my fingers. "You can't *do* that!"

He gives me a lazy, heated grin. "Why not?"

With his hair slicked back and his posture so relaxed, he's the image of sin. And his arm is still moving in sinuous, slow jerks.

Just how thoroughly is he washing that—that thing?

"Wash yourself, Dawn," he purrs. "I don't mind."

I sink to my neck again and keep my suspicious gaze on him. If he so much as breathes in my direction, I'll poke him in the eye. Which is silly, considering that he was so very close earlier when he washed my hair. But with this orc, I seem to oscillate from one extreme to the other, wanting him close one moment and hating the thought of his touch the next.

Slowly, careful not to disturb the water, I reach between my legs and give myself a tentative stroke.

It's just washing. You've done it a thousand times before.

But it's not. Not when Gorvor stills on his side of the pool, every ounce of his attention trained on me. I attempt another swipe, and he groans softly, his shoulders bunching with tension.

"How does it feel?" he asks in a low voice.

"What?" I still with my hand on my belly, confusion coursing through me.

He leans forward, though he doesn't leave his spot. "How does it feel when you tease yourself?"

"Um." I push my damp hair away from my face, unsure of what he's talking about. "Tease myself?"

The king narrows his eyes at me. "Are you a virgin?"

"No," I reply truthfully.

I'd sold that *privilege* to a rich merchant's son when he and his father had stayed at the inn where I'd worked. The last winter had been bitter and long, and my wages from sweeping the rooms, emptying chamber pots, and washing bed linens were barely enough to keep me fed. I'd wanted a new cloak and a pair of good leather boots, lined with wool, so I'd bargained with the young fool and won enough money to buy a scarf and mittens, too. I didn't care about being intact for my future husband, because I'd had no intention of marrying anyone. I only got whatever I could in exchange for it.

Now I worry for the first time that this orc might have expected his bride to be innocent on what has become our wedding night, for all intents and purposes.

But Gorvor gives me a satisfied nod. "Good. So what did the men you slept with do to make you ready for them?"

I clear my throat. "There was just the one man. And he hiked up my skirts and, well..."

I motion with my hand to indicate that he'd wedged

himself between my legs and rutted there for a short period of time before collapsing with a grunt. I'd felt some discomfort, a pinching pain, but it hadn't been too horrible. My whispered conversations with the other maids have taught me that my experience was much the norm. Sexual relations are an unpleasant but sometimes necessary burden, and as long as we drink our special teas and don't get pregnant, it isn't much to talk about.

Gorvor drags his palm over his face. "No wonder you don't want me to touch you."

I raise my eyebrows at him.

He leans against the edge but keeps his burning gaze on me. "Human men keep their women ignorant and unsatisfied, and yet you tell stories about how backward orcs are, aye?"

I scoot back on the underwater ledge, wondering where he's going with this. "Maybe?"

"I will not touch you until you beg me to," he rumbles. "But will you touch yourself if I teach you?"

"Touch myself?" I swallow, worry rising in me again. "How?"

"Trust me, Dawn," he replies. "Just for this?"

I nod, unsure of what he's talking about. Because I do trust him. A warm sensation has sprouted up in my chest, something new and unexpected. Every promise this orc has made me, he has kept, which is more than I can say for most humans I've met in my life—male or female.

"Good," Gorvor says. "Now bring your hand back between your legs."

Shivering despite the warm water, I obey his order. I keep my gaze on him, tracking his movements to see where this is going.

"If you slip your fingers between your lower lips, you'll feel how slick you are there," he continues.

I do as he says, trailing my middle finger through my most intimate place.

"Just like that," he growls.

I gasp as realization hits me. "You can see what I'm doing?"

His grin is broad and unrepentant. "Orcs see much better than humans."

"Oh!" I wrap one arm around my naked breasts and cover my sex with my other hand. "You—you—"

"You're beautiful, Dawn," he says. "Never hide yourself from me. Remember, you said you trusted me. Let me make you feel good."

The intensity of his voice melts some of my embarrassment. He sounds so earnest about this, I'm getting more and more curious about what he could mean.

"What do I do now?" I ask, and my words come out soft, inquisitive.

The king gives me an approving look. "At the top of your pussy, you'll find a little bud. A sensitive pearl of flesh. Run your finger lightly over it."

I bite my lip as I follow his instructions. The expressions he's using are crude, but I don't mind. This is my body, and exploring it feels nice. And there, right where he said it would be, is a small, tight pearl, as he'd called it. I circle it with my fingertip, and a shudder runs through my limbs. "Oh!"

"Perfect," he murmurs. "Now stay there. And do with it what feels good. Maybe you'll want to press down. Or flick it. Or rub over it. Try. Now."

The low timbre of his voice is almost hypnotic, and I do as he says until I find the right amount of pressure, the right rhythm. My legs part on their own, and a new, delicious warmth spreads from my core.

"Keep doing that," he says. "The pleasure will build."

"It's building," I gasp. "I like it, Gorvor."

Another tremor shakes me, and I close my eyes, letting my head fall back on the edge of the pool.

"Open your eyes, little mate."

The king's voice sounds closer. I glance up to find him standing in the middle of the pool. Almost close enough to touch. The water covers him to his chest, but I can still see the movements of his right arm, rhythmic and jerky.

"What are *you* doing?" I ask, breathless.

"I'm jerking my cock, watching you," he growls. "You are so damn beautiful."

Jerking his—oh gods, why is this so good?

"Does it feel like what I'm doing?" I force myself to keep my eyes open, not wanting to miss even a second of this.

He hisses a breath through his teeth. "Aye. I want to sink my cock in your pretty little pussy. You'd take me so well, Dawn. All of me. But not tonight because you need to do this for yourself."

The pressure inside me rises, and I thrash my head from side to side, wanting something I can't name, can't reach.

"Gorvor, I need—" I frown at him, desperate. "I don't know what I need!"

"Shh," he says, slowing the movements of his hand. "Take your other hand between your legs. And push a finger into your pussy."

"*Into* it?" My voice hitches over those words. "But—"

"*Trust me*," he urges, forcing the command out through his teeth. "Do it now."

Trembling with anticipation, I slowly slide my middle finger through my folds. The intrusion feels strange for a moment but not unpleasant. Nothing like the time when that man—no, that *boy*—did it. My pussy is slick and hot, and so, so sensitive.

Gorvor says, "Now hook your finger forward."

I frown in concentration. It's hard keeping up with my other hand and doing this as well, and I'm about to tell him that, but at that moment, I touch some hidden spot inside me that has every muscle in my body locking up.

I open my mouth on a silent moan, and when I repeat the movement, my vision tunnels from pleasure until Gorvor is all I see.

"Oh gods!" I roll my finger pad over my bud, faster and faster. "I can't take any more of this."

"You can. Don't stop."

He crowds in next to me, but I'm so far gone I don't mind it anymore. He runs his nose over my temple and drags in a breath. The deep growl that reverberates through the room loosens something inside me. Gorvor's jerks quicken, his harsh breaths heating my skin.

Then a bright ball of pleasure bursts in my core, and I cry out in shock and delight. My pussy squeezes around my finger, and another flick over my pearl sends me flying. It's the most exquisite feeling I've ever experienced, and I have nothing to compare it with. I rock my hips over and over, prolonging it as much as I can because I don't want to let it go.

Next to me, Gorvor snarls and hunches his shoulders, his big body shaking. If his...*finish* was anything like mine, I'm surprised he's still standing. Suddenly, I'm curious to see him do this out of the water, where I could witness what goes into making this hard, serious man lose his composure.

The king hums softly and draws me into his arms. My

body feels loose and heavy, with sparks of pleasure still dancing through my veins. The warm slide of his skin against mine is incredible, so I wind my arms around Gorvor's neck and let him lift me from the water. His expression doesn't change, but that new awareness inside my chest blooms stronger.

He sets me on his bed and wraps a large bath sheet around me and another one around his waist. I'm too tired to protest, but disappointment lances through me when he hides himself from my view.

Tomorrow, then.

I never thought I'd end up like this, but at this moment, I can't bring myself to regret it. Not when Gorvor gently rubs my skin with the linen cloth, nor when he sits behind me and passes a coarse comb through my hair. He gives me privacy to use the toilet hidden behind what I thought was a wall tapestry, a small nook with more running water that washes away all the unpleasantness. And I certainly don't complain when he helps me lie on his bed, on the soft mattress, and covers me with a light wool blanket.

"Sleep well, little mate," he murmurs.

The last thing I know before sleep takes me under is the shifting of the bed on the other side.

CHAPTER

SIX

It's been years since I've slept so well. My usual nightmares didn't plague me at all. I'm warm, lying on something soft and comfortable, and the room is still dark, which means I haven't overslept for once. I know I'll have to get up soon and start work, but if I can get a moment of rest more, I'll take it.

A hot exhale on my face is the first indication that I'm not in my own bed anymore. In a dizzying rush, everything that has happened in the past weeks comes crashing back, and I stiffen in place. The only explanation for the warmth I'm currently experiencing is...

The orc king.

I pry one eye open and find myself staring at a vast expanse of skin. Green, taut skin that covers the inhumanly large muscles of Gorvor's chest. Because I am plastered to his side, and the warm pillow I thought I was resting on is actually his chest. My arm is draped over his belly, which rises and falls with each long breath, and my leg is hooked over his hip, brushing up against something hard and heavy.

Oh gods.

It's worse than I imagined. I'd thought that maybe he'd taken advantage of me, groping me in my sleep, but no— I'm clinging to him while he rests peacefully. While we're both naked. Completely, utterly naked.

Not that he seems to mind. As if sensing my agitation, the king shifts in his sleep and rubs his cheek over the top of my head. He curves the arm I'm lying on and grips my naked waist, drawing me closer to his side.

I need to escape. A moment to gather my thoughts, and I'll be cured of whatever madness possessed me to allow this to happen.

Then the memory of what we did in the giant bathtub surfaces, and I settle down again. The sensations I'd experienced were unlike anything I've ever felt, and my insides clench as I think of repeating it. It's no wonder men are so obsessed with sex. If my interlude with the merchant's son was anything like last night's moment with Gorvor, I'd be chasing the poor idiot down and insisting we get married. It's probably lucky that he didn't give me this kind of high. I didn't like him, and I wouldn't have wanted to be his wife.

Instead, I seem to have become this orc's mate.

Trying to be stealthy, I peel my arm and leg off Gorvor and push myself into a seated position. Maybe I can get dressed and ready before he wakes up and demands anything from me. But I pause, staring down at him. The conflicting impulses inside me are waging war against each other—the proper, human-bred instinct to cover myself and the curious part of me that wants to know *more*.

More about this orc male who kept his promises last night. More about my own body—because he seems to know it better than I do, and that's unacceptable.

I must be mad, because I let the curiosity win. Biting my

lip, I slowly tug on the linen sheet that's covering Gorvor's cock. It feels scandalous to call it that, even in my mind, but that's what he called it last night, so I want to, as well.

My brain stutters to a stop. The king is so much bigger than me, than any human, of course, so it makes sense that his cock is larger than a human's. But compared to what I'd briefly seen between that human boy's legs, this is...

Frightening.

I'd felt my pussy last night when Gorvor had guided me to pleasure myself with my finger. There is no possible way this thick member would ever fit inside me.

The large, green cock twitches slightly, growing more erect before my eyes. The shaft thickens, and the head distends, but the most amazing thing about it is the bulbous shape at the bottom, something I definitely didn't see with that human guy.

What does it do?

The cock rises all on its own, jutting up at an angle, and I have to curb the sudden desire to *touch*.

"Do you like it?"

I jump, fumbling with the sheets. Gorvor lies still, exactly as before, but his dark eyes are open, and he wears that crooked, dry grin I'd admired last night.

"Oh!" I cover my breasts with one arm and drape my hair forward to help me hide my nudity. "I didn't know you were— I didn't mean to—"

One warm palm lands on my lower back, and Gorvor rubs slow, soothing circles on my naked skin. "No need to fret, little mate. You can look as much as you want."

"I wasn't *looking*." I lift my chin, but I don't move away from his touch. It feels good, and I like it.

The king chuckles. "No? Well, you can look now."

50

I try to avert my gaze, I do. But it's just so *large*. Biting my lip, I glance over to it again, fascinated despite myself.

"You're worried," he rumbles. "About how it will fit?"

Peeking up at him again, I give him a tiny nod. Not that I'm thinking about having sex with him. But the mechanics are…intriguing.

The pressure of his hand increases slightly, and he brushes it lower, over the top of my ass. No man has ever touched me like that. He traces the bumps of my spine with his thumb, then curls his fingers around my hip, giving the rounded, soft part of me a squeeze.

"If I tried to fuck you without making sure you were ready," he begins, "I would hurt you. That's true."

I swallow thickly. "But—you won't."

It's not really a question, not after last night when he'd kept his word.

"No, I won't, Dawn." He continues his slow exploration of me, almost absentmindedly, like he enjoys touching me but isn't paying attention. "I will make sure you're slick and wet for me."

His fingers brush the side of my breast, and my nipples pebble into hard, aching points. Maybe that's why I dare to voice my next question.

"How?"

His gaze sharpens. "You want me to show you?"

My hands tremble as I lower them, letting him see all of me. "Maybe. But not—not *that*." I glance at his huge cock. "Um, not yet."

Smiling wolfishly, he replies, "Oh, no, you're not getting that. Not until you beg."

I bristle at the implication that I would ever beg for sex. But then—perhaps I would. If it was as good as what I experienced last night, maybe Gorvor could reduce me to begging. I will never know until I try.

The king doesn't pounce on me like I expected. He continues that sensuous stroking, caressing my skin. He pauses on my ass and slips lower, cupping me with his big palm. I squirm in place.

He smiles wider, his tusks glimmering in the low light. "Easy."

I want to demand that he speed up. This waiting is excruciating, but instead of giving in to my impatience, I resist.

"Good," Gorvor purrs. "Now lie on your back."

Shivering, I do as he asks. He rears above me, and a spike of fear shoots through me. He could so easily force me to do what he wants—or crush me. But the steady, heated look in his eyes tells me he's not about to go feral and hurt me. For some reason, this orc is intent on showing me what I've been missing out on, and I want to let him.

"First, I'd make love to your mouth." He lowers his head and brushes his nose over my cheek, inhaling. "You smell so good."

I brace my palms on his chest—not that I could push him off, even if I tried—but I need an anchor, and his warm skin and the shifting muscles beneath it are so appealing. His scent invades my senses, scrambling my thoughts, or maybe that's the way he presses slow kisses to my jaw, my cheek, the corner of my mouth.

Then he kisses me, and it's the first *real* kiss I've ever experienced. Yes, I've had pecks and fumbling, sloppy kisses, but this puts them all to shame. Gorvor takes my lips with complete confidence, his tongue slipping in to caress mine. I'd been afraid his tusks would get in the way, but they're just a part of him. I return each kiss as best I can. I slip my hands around his neck and hold him close, and Gorvor makes a pleased, growling sound in his throat that spurs me on even further. I open for him, allowing him to plunder my mouth, and the warmth from his kiss melts the rest of my reluctance.

He chuckles deeply and moves on from my mouth, and I protest, fisting his long hair and dragging him back for another kiss. That sensation inside me intensifies, as if some bond has formed between us that relishes our closeness.

"You wanted me to show you something," he says between kisses. "But now you want me to kiss you all morning?"

"Mm," I hum. "Can't we do both?"

"We could," he replies. "But not today. Right now, I need you wet and hot and not afraid."

When he lifts his head, his expression is serious. So I give him a small nod and loosen my fingers from his hair. He kisses my neck, my shoulder, and travels down to my breasts. I squeak and try to cover them with my hands, but he shakes his head, takes my wrists, and pins them to either side of my head.

"No hiding, Dawn." His words are rough, a sharp command. "We don't hide from each other."

"All right," I breathe.

He lets me go and leans down to take my nipple in his mouth. I gasp, squirming under him, and he teases me, sucking and licking. He brings his palm up to my other breast and pinches my nipple between his fingers. He rolls and tugs on it, and every touch sends pleasure straight to my core, building pressure that needs release.

"Gorvor," I pant, "please."

I don't know what I'm asking for, apart from wishing for that glorious feeling I experienced last night.

"I'll take care of you," he promises. "I can smell how wet you are already."

Embarrassment rises in me, and I try to close my legs, but he has wedged himself between them.

He raises his head from my breasts and sends me a stern look. "What did we say?"

"Don't stop," I beg.

He keeps me in suspense and remains still. Instead, he raises one black eyebrow, waiting for my words.

Finally, I cave and spread my thighs wider. "No hiding."

"Good girl," he rumbles. "That's it."

Without warning, he pinches both of my nipples, and I cry out, my back arching off the bed. I don't know if it's possible to achieve that blissful feeling with him just teasing my nipples, but I need him lower, *now*.

With a dark laugh, he rains kisses over my soft belly, and with the way he dips his tongue in my navel, I get the first idea of what he intends to do.

"Oh," I gasp when he digs his strong fingers in my thighs and hikes them up. "I don't know—"

His hot breath falls on my pussy, and words desert me. I'm all trembling anticipation and awkwardness, worried he might not like what he sees down there.

But Gorvor's dark gaze meets mine for a brief second. "You're gorgeous. All over. So wet for me already, and I haven't even touched you yet."

"You have," I protest. "You've done *plenty* of touch—*ah!*"

I yelp as he runs one blunt fingertip through my pussy, spreading the slickness over my lower lips. He doesn't push inside me or touch my pearl, and the anticipation has me shifting my hips again, until he pins me down with one hand, sending me an admonishing glower.

"I told you I'd show you how I'd get you ready for me," he says. "This is how."

A tremble starts in my chest, a shiver of expectation I can't seem to calm. "Gorvor, please. I don't know what to do."

He rears up and presses a rough, possessive kiss on my mouth. "You don't have to do anything. Let go for me."

He slowly pushes his big finger inside me, and I take him easily, slippery as I am. I glance down my body, and the sight of his green-skinned hand against my pussy is so erotic, I gasp, feeling almost as if this is happening to someone else. Surely, this kind of pleasure doesn't exist in my world, not when I'm—

"Dawn," the king says. "Look at me."

I lift my gaze to his face, which is taut with tension. Our eyes locked, we stare at each other as he feeds another finger inside me, stretching me. My eyelids flutter, but I don't look away. He's telling me something with every touch, every heated kiss.

I'm here. This is no dream, no illusion. This scarred, powerful male wants *me*. The heavy weight of his cock rests against my hip, and he rocks up slightly, like he can't help himself. At the same time, he fucks me with slow strokes of his fingers, hooking them up like he'd instructed me last night.

The pressure inside me builds, but I need more—I don't know if I can finish just from him teasing my pussy.

I open my mouth to tell him that, but he gives me that wicked grin and lowers himself between my legs again.

"What are you doing?" I ask, craning my neck.

"Eyes on me," he commands. "I want you to see everything."

With that, he plunges his fingers deeper inside me and runs his tongue over my bundle of nerves. The sensation is so shockingly intense, I cry out and try to squeeze my legs shut, but he's there, he's so big and rude and coarse, and he's making me feel things I've never experienced before, and I hate him a little for it.

"Shh," he murmurs. "Should I stop?"

"No!" I throw my head back and cover my face with my arm. "Do it again."

His chuckle fans hot breath over my pussy. "Do what, Dawn?"

Oh, the evil, wicked orc.

I lower my arm and glare at him. "Lick me."

And he does. He does exactly what I ask of him and drags the flat of his hot tongue over my pearl again and again, then latches his lips on it and sucks. And I scream, pleasure breaking over me in waves, each thrust of his thick fingers prolonging my climax. Gorvor pushes a third finger into my squeezing pussy, and the feeling is incredible.

"See how well you take me," he growls. "You'll take my cock as well."

He caresses me until I shiver and melt back into the sheets, spent and satisfied. Then he pulls his hand away, brings his fingers to his mouth, and licks my wetness off them.

I gasp at the lewdness of it, but he grins at me, satisfaction clear on his face.

"You taste like honey," he says. "I knew you would."

With all that pleasure coursing through me, I can't even be properly outraged. "You're terrible."

He reaches between my legs again and swipes his fingers through my slick folds. "Ah, but good, too?"

I bite my lip and look up at him. "Yes. Very good."

This time, he doesn't lick his fingers clean. Instead, he wraps his hand around his cock and gives himself a firm stroke from root to tip. He hisses and sits back on his heels, displaying himself for me. "Will you watch me?"

I scramble upright and push my hair away from my face. "Yes."

He jerks his hand over his cock in hard, almost rough movements. With his other hand, he palms the bulge at the bottom, squeezing it in time with his strokes.

"What is that?" I ask, drawing closer.

Gorvor slows and moves his hand to let me see. "My knot. You'll take it when we fuck, and it'll lock inside you, keeping us together."

The thought of it draws a gasp from my lips. "For how long?"

He strokes his cock again, and a drop of his cum appears on the tip of his thick head, creamy and white. For some reason, my mouth waters at the sight, and I lift my gaze up to the king's face before I do anything stupid. Like lick it.

"I don't know," he admits. "No one has ever taken my knot."

I stare at him. "No one? You've never...fucked anyone before?"

I force myself to use the words he's using, to name the act without embarrassment.

Gorvor gives me a dark chuckle in answer. "I have. But only my mate can take my knot."

Oh my.

The thought of him pleasuring some other woman fills me with irrational, burning jealousy. I want to wipe those women from his mind and only have him think of me. He didn't even want a human mate—he'd said as much when he'd first brought me to his room. But I'm here, and now that I've experienced what he has to give, I'm not so keen on leaving anymore.

"Can I try?" I ask, not wanting to lose my nerve. "Touching you, I mean?"

Gorvor's mouth opens on a harsh exhale. "Aye. You are my mate. And I am yours."

That statement fills me with so much vicious satisfaction. No one else will do this. This hard cock is all for me, and I will learn to bring him as much pleasure as he did to me. Because I want him to feel like I do—breathless with want. Trembling for a touch.

"Show me how," I tell him.

The king takes my hands and wraps one around his shaft, the other around his knot. He squeezes to show me how much pressure he wants, and I imitate his movements until he growls in approval, his hips rocking up lightly.

"You're so thick," I whisper in awe.

My fingers can't even reach all the way around his shaft, let alone the knot at the bottom. But for once, I'm not afraid—if he says I can take him, I believe him. I stroke my palm up his cock and swipe my thumb over the wetness at the tip, spreading it around to slick my palm. At the same time, I squeeze his knot, feeling the tension inside it. To have that locked in my pussy... It would keep us together, trapping his semen inside me.

And gods, the thought is erotic, forbidden.

I gaze up at Gorvor to find him staring down at me, his lips parted, his stern brow furrowed. He looks like he's in pain, and I slow my movements, worry coursing through me that I've somehow messed up.

"Don't stop," he grinds out through clenched teeth.

Then he takes me by the back of my neck and hauls me in for a kiss, a claiming that has me whimpering into his mouth. He drinks in the sound, and it's like something snaps inside him, some tether that has been holding him back. He lifts me easily in his arms, his hands splayed on my ass, and pulls me in so our bodies are flush. Jerking his hips into my tight grip, he fucks my hands over and over while rocking me in the same rhythm, as if he's imagining plunging inside my pussy.

His cock thickens in my hand, and then he's coming, spurting his seed all over my hands, my belly, my breasts. He roars, throwing his head back. The tendons straining in his neck are the most beautiful thing I've ever seen.

I caused this. I made him come apart, and it's glorious. Last night, he did this to himself, but I was too absorbed in my own sensations to really notice. Now I take stock of every little detail—the rise and fall of his massive chest, the sticky warmth of his cum, the possessive squeeze of his fingers on my ass.

Slowly, his breathing returns to normal, and he drops his head to my shoulder on a long exhale. His cock, semi-hard in my grip, seems spent, and suddenly, I don't know what to do. I should clean myself off, but he's still holding me, and I don't want him to know how I feel. He would probably laugh if he knew I'm putting so much value in a simple act of bringing each other pleasure.

Only there's nothing simple about it. I've never done anything like this, and it feels like my world has shifted. That I trusted him with my body, with my safety, is incredible for me, and I'm not sure how to express that with words.

"Oh, little mate." Gorvor slowly lets go of me and deposits me on the bed. "Come on. Let's wash together."

It turns out I needn't have worried. From the way he wraps his arm around my shoulders and tucks me into his side, to how he helps me into the bathing pool and gently washes my body, the king shows me with his actions what human men try and fail to say with their flowery speeches and poetry. He's patient with me, and by the time we're done, I'm almost ready for another round of pleasure-making.

But he helps me put on my dress and ties the laces in the back. His deep-brown leather pants and weapons belt are a perfect outfit for a warrior, but this time, he doesn't bother with his linen tunic.

"We are going on a hunt," he informs me. "I will see you again in the evening."

I stare at him, apprehension rising in me. "Am I not going with you?"

He lifts one eyebrow. "Can you hunt?"

I shake my head, almost embarrassed to admit it. My life back in the human world would have been much easier if I'd mastered the craft. I could have provided for myself.

"Then you're not coming," he says, his words final.

He opens a chest, draws out several daggers, and sheaths them on his weapons belt. Next comes his quiver of arrows, which he slings on his naked back, and a wicked-looking curved knife with an intricately carved bone handle. The king stands, picks up an unstrung bow from its holder on the wall, and walks over to me.

"See you tonight, little mate."

He leans down and inhales deeply, rubbing his cheek against mine. It's an intimate gesture, comforting without being sexual, and my poor, neglected heart gives a lurch.

Without thinking, I go up on my tiptoes and press a quick kiss to his jaw. He gives me a warm smile and leaves, closing the door softly behind him.

The room sinks into silence, the earthen walls dampening all sound. I'm alone for the first time in weeks, so I sit on the edge of the bed and stare at the tapestry covering the privy niche.

First, my throat closes up, and I swallow to get rid of the sensation, but it won't budge. My life has been turned on its head, and I haven't had even a moment's peace to process it all. My eyes sting with hot tears, so I dash the edge of my sleeve over them, but it doesn't help.

When will the king show his true nature? His words are surely deceitful, and they have me feeling things I have no business even thinking about. I've heard the stories. Orcs aren't kind. They aren't gentle. They take what they want by force, and doubting their ways will only bring me more grief later. It's likely only a matter of time before he snaps and hurts me.

The tears come, fast and silent. I curl up on the king's bed, his delicious scent rising around me, and I cry—for myself, for all the fear I've experienced, for the strange feelings that Gorvor has evoked in me.

My life will never be the same.

And I don't know what to do.

SEVEN

A knock on the door wakes me from a fitful nap. I'd cried myself into a stupor and fell asleep sniffling into Gorvor's pillow. I raise my head, groggy and puffy-eyed.

"Who is it?" I call.

The door opens a crack, and an orc woman pokes her head into the room. "Hello?"

It's the young stranger who hugged me yesterday—the king's cousin.

I give her a weak wave. "I'm over here."

She takes one glance at me, and her large brown eyes widen in shock. "Oh dear."

I must look frightening if even an orc is appalled by my appearance.

The thought shoots through my mind, and is immediately followed by shame. The orc woman standing in the doorway is...beautiful. She's not handsome by human standards, maybe, but her tall, curvy body is stately, her bosom accentuated by her lovely dress, and her green skin is clear and glowing. Her doe eyes are stunning, and her long black braid is expertly plaited. She radiates health in a sturdy, fertile sort of way, and suddenly, I'm embarrassed about my unbound hair, my swollen face, and my wrinkled dress.

She says something to the guards still stationed outside, steps into the room, and closes the door behind her. Then she walks right to the bed and sits on the edge next to me.

"Are you all right?" she asks softly.

I force myself to sit up and rake my fingers through my hair in an attempt to tame it. "Yes. I'm fine."

She raises her eyebrow, and in that moment, she resembles the king so much, I can't continue pretending I haven't recognized her.

"You're Gorvor's cousin," I say, straightening my spine. "You brought me dresses yesterday."

Her smile lights up her face. "I'm Mara."

"I'm Dawn." I stick my hand out, then realize what I'm doing. "Gods, I'm meeting his family while lying in bed. I'm sorry."

I make a move to stand, but she puts a hand on my arm to stop me.

"Don't get up. I find beds to be so comfortable, don't you?" She pats the pillow and gives me an encouraging smile.

I bite my lip. "All right, but I do have to wash my face. Wait here."

She settles in, and I dash to where the water pitcher sits on a chest and splash my face with cold water. I take Gorvor's comb and run it through my hair, then hastily braid it. I brush my hands over the skirt of my dress and sigh, resigned to the wrinkles. This is the best I can do without time to prepare.

I return to bed and perch next to Mara. "So, did the king send you to check up on me?"

The corner of her lips turns up. "He asked me to show you around the Hill, but if you'd rather stay here, we can send one of the guards for some honey cakes from the kitchens and I can tell you all the clan gossip."

That startles a surprised laugh from me. "That sounds like an amazing idea, but I should probably learn my way around so I'm not completely dependent on others."

A voice inside my head is insisting I should milk this woman for information, make sure I have an escape plan formulated in case I decide to leave rather than take my chances with the king. But until I know more about the settlement and the lands surrounding it, any attempt at running away would end in my capture—or I'd get lost in the woods and die of exposure.

Mara hops from the bed and offers me her arm. "What do you want to see first?"

She throws open the door, and the two guards stand at attention. I recognize both from last night, and I wonder if they've been standing here all this time. I hope not.

"Vark, Steagor," I greet them, and they bow in return.

Then Vark presents me with a lit lantern, a beautifully crafted silvery one with clear glass protecting the oil-fueled flame inside. "The king requested one of these for you. He says your human eyes are too poor to see in the dark. Is that true?"

Mara smacks the guard's shoulder, hard. "For shame! You can't say that to your queen."

Vark looks properly chastened, and he gives me another deep bow. "Forgive me, my lady."

I can't help but grin. "It's fine. And it's true that human eyesight is very poor in the dark."

Through all this, Steagor remains silent and grim, his

hand on one of the several short-handled hatchets hanging from his waist.

Vark turns to him as if he'd been contributing to the conversation all along. "You were right. This would mean a significant advantage when fighting humans."

Mara tugs my hand, and we start down the corridor in the direction Gorvor and I took last night, toward the great hall.

"Do orcs often fight with humans?" I murmur.

I meant the question for Mara, but apparently, orc hearing is also better than human, because it's Vark who answers from behind us.

"Aye, my lady. They sometimes come and try to take back the humans we save from auction houses." He lets out a snort. "But they leave quickly when they realize the humans want to stay."

I glance over my shoulder at him. "So there are other humans here? But you haven't met any to know of our...shortcomings?"

He laughs, a booming, cheerful sound that reverberates through the corridor. "You are short, that's true." He reaches out and pats my shoulder, his palm warm. "There are very few humans in this settlement. Several live in our outer villages, though, because they were mated with orcs who live there."

I hide my surprise at him touching me. I was definitely not part of the nobility in the human world, but if I was, a guard would lose his hand if he dared lay it on the queen, even for a friendly gesture like this. Strangely enough, I find myself not hating the contact. It makes me feel more like one of the crowd. If all orcs are this free-thinking when it comes to nudity, touching, and relationships, I might not want to go back to the human world either.

There's more I need to know, however. No one has tried to hurt me yet, but they did buy me at auction. And I certainly didn't agree to being mated with their king, no matter how much I've enjoyed my interactions with him since. I'm torn between wanting more of their hospitality and being offended on principle because they keep making decisions for me.

"Why do you even take humans?" I ask, stopping in the dark corridor. "Why *buy* us? Shouldn't we be given the choice to come here?"

The pool of light cast by my lantern creates long shadows in the dark underground corridor. The three orcs, all taller than me, look even stranger in this yellow glow, and yet they're staring at me like I've grown another head.

"Dawn, we save people like you," Mara says slowly. "The king has been working for years to end slavery. Think for a moment. You were at the auction house, and if Neekar and Ozork hadn't purchased you, where do you think you would have ended up?"

My mouth goes dry at the thought, but I give her a truthful answer. "Probably in a brothel somewhere. Or as some depraved rich man's sex slave."

She reaches out and rubs my arm, the gesture comforting. "And now you're here. You've found your true mate. You're safe."

My true mate.

Gorvor had insisted I was his mate, but I hadn't considered what that meant for *me*. Was he mine as well? He'd claimed as much, but I couldn't entirely believe that he was my perfect match.

Why not?

I'd had no luck in the human world, despite having

lived there for more than twenty-six years. So why shouldn't my life's companion be an orc?

"Why didn't they let me go, though?" I whisper. "The warriors. They bundled me up in a cart and wouldn't let me return to my village."

Vark frowns down at me. "You wanted to return? The orcs who travel to town are told to make sure the ones they bring here have no ties back to the human lands."

I open my mouth to answer, then close it again. A memory surges up from the day I was freed from the slave barracks in Ultrup. Of Ozork lifting me into the wagon and asking me in his gruff way if there was a home I could go back to. I'd sobbed and told him I had no home.

What I'd said was the truth. The men who'd kidnapped me grabbed me from an alley by the inn where I'd been working—and sleeping in the servants' quarters. It was no home, that's for sure, even though I'd found some kind people there.

I'd been lucky, so lucky, that the slavers hadn't raped me or worse. They'd seemed to know that I would fetch a higher price if I wasn't brutalized, so they'd merely bound me and tossed me in the back of the cart, where I'd shared the filthy space with a goat and four chickens they must have stolen, too. To them, I'd been a thing, an object to be sold.

Mara seems to realize that I have no good answer to Vark's inquiry. She takes my hand and leads me onward, and I follow, still lost in memories. If what she and Vark are saying is true, then Ozork, Neekar, and the rest of the warriors aren't horrible monsters at all. They'd simply brought me here because they didn't know where else to take me.

And I'd somehow ended up being mated to their king.

"What happens if a human isn't mated to anyone?" I ask as the noise from the great hall reaches my ears. "Are they returned?"

Mara shakes her head. "Not if they don't want to leave. Depending on their age and skill, they take up work where they can. Orcs are good at a lot of things, but not every skill or craft out there." She motions at my dress. "Like sewing. We are mostly horrible at things that require a lot of precision."

I smile at the memory of how frustrated Gorvor had been with the laces of my dress. "I can imagine that."

We enter the great hall, and orcs greet us, exchanging back slaps, handshakes, and even hugs with my three companions. I receive several pats on my shoulders and a motherly embrace from an older orc woman who squeezes me against her large bosom that smells of chamomile and lavender. Mara introduces her as Taris, their herbalist, and she loudly informs me that she has prepared a tea for me that will make the king's seed plant much quicker in my womb.

All the orcs within earshot cheer loudly at this, but I duck my head, embarrassed beyond words at the thought of discussing my womb—or the king's seed—with anyone out in the open.

"Do they all think we're going to have babies?" I whisper at Mara, panicking. "Straight away? I only met him last night!"

Not that this fact prevented us from enjoying each other's bodies, of course. Maybe that's the effect of the mate bond. The attraction and desire, the strange trust that formed between us. Gorvor, despite being much larger and stronger than me, must have trusted me, too, to let me sleep in his bed. If he hadn't, he could have given me any of the other rooms in the underground settlement. But he'd taken me to his bed and shown me pleasure and kindness.

My mind swims with confusion. Mara tugs me to one of the tables, not the one where I'd sat with the king last night but a regular one, where a family of orcs seems to be finishing their lunch. I sit next to the mother and give her a small smile, and she grins back and hands me a basket of bread. Her belly is rounded with pregnancy, and her mate waits on her, bringing her more tea and fussing around, asking her whether she wants more fruit. She bears it all with remarkable patience.

Their two children, little twin boys, climb their father's shoulders and jabber excitedly, pointing at me. I sit very still as they toddle over to me and touch my hands and pat my braided brown hair, as if I'm the first human they've ever seen and they find me interesting.

"That's enough," the father booms at last. "Leave the lady to eat in peace."

I glance from him to his mate. "I don't mind. They're beautiful boys."

"Thank you," the woman says simply.

They clear the table and take their dishes to the kitchens, and I watch them leave, a strange kind of longing blooming inside my chest.

"You're good with children," Mara says, startling me from my thoughts.

I turn to find her and both guards watching me. "Oh, right. They were so adorable."

I don't know why seeing orc children changes so much in how I view their entire people, but it docs. I'd noticed a couple of kids running around at dinner last night, but seeing their pudgy little hands, their tiny tusks, and their delicate pointed ears up close brought home the realization that this isn't some den of bandits but a thriving, living community. Orcs of all ages live here, families, elderly couples, and yes, warriors as well.

My knowledge of their culture and traditions is horribly incomplete. They accepted me without question, and I've insulted them. I hope I haven't done any irreparable damage yet.

"Will you show me around?" I quietly ask Mara. "I want to learn more."

She gives me an encouraging smile. "Right after you eat something. My cousin would never forgive me if I let his mate starve under my watch."

We eat together, and afterward, the guards escort us all through the underground dwelling, from the great hall to the kitchens and beyond. We visit the stables and the infirmary, where I meet the first human, an older man with a sour face who asks if I'm squeamish about blood. When I tell him no, he gives me a stern look and tells me to be ready for his call.

Mara ushers me out and pats my hand. "Don't worry about our healer. He is convinced orcs are idiots for not wearing armor to battle and keeps insisting he's done sewing up our warriors."

Vark snorts. "An orc's greatest strength is his speed and agility. Anyone can smash around with his sword. The trick is not getting struck."

I think of the scars marring the king's chest and shoulders and wonder what happened to him if that's true. I doubt the orcs would tolerate him as their king if he wasn't a great warrior, so what had caused all his injuries?

The list of questions I want to ask Gorvor gets longer as the day progresses. There is much to be seen, from the underwater stream and the gardens filled with glowing mushrooms, to the school where orc children of various ages are being taught their letters by a patient young orc woman. They take me to the communal hot baths—because apparently only the king and a few select individuals have thermal pools in their own rooms—and I lay eyes on more naked orcs than I ever wanted to see. Everywhere we go, Mara introduces me, and I try to remember everyone's names, repeating them to myself.

In one of the corridors, we meet a scout party returning from the forest, three tall orcs who move through the halls soundlessly, as if they're still stalking their prey. They disappear down a long tunnel to our right, and I stop, staring after them. As much as I tried to keep up with all the twists and turns, I think I might have gotten lost, because I'm fairly sure we haven't explored anything in the direction these males are going.

"What's that way?" I take a step after them.

But Steagor puts himself in my way, his bulky body all but filling the corridor from top to bottom.

"Uh, just some storage rooms," Mara says quickly. She takes my arm and guides me back the way we were walking before. "The Hill is riddled with tunnels. You have to take care that you don't get lost."

Her words make sense, and yet there's something in her expression that gives me pause. Whatever is down that corridor seems to be off-limits for me.

I cast a look over my shoulder at my guards. "There's not much chance of that, is there?"

Because despite all their talk of offering me freedom, I'm still not allowed to go off on my own. My ever-present shadows, however polite, make my status in this clan quite clear. If I ever decide on running away after all, I'm not sure they'll let me.

When I trip over my own feet despite the lantern, Steagor steps in and offers to carry me back to the king's quarters. I decline his suggestion, not wanting to seem weak, but I feel like I've made a good impression on the gruff warrior—he's barely spoken all day, so this seems like progress.

Still, I'm not sorry to see that we're returning to the corridor I now recognize as the one leading to Gorvor's room. Just before we reach the right door, however, Vark, who is walking in front, suddenly stops. His posture changes, and for the first time that day, he reaches with both hands to his weapons belt and grasps the handles of two long daggers.

"What's going on?" I ask, peering around his bulky shoulders.

Right in front of the king's door, two orcs stand talking quietly. They fall silent at our approach and turn to face us. I immediately recognize the male who gave that strange speech at dinner last night and one of his companions, both wearing the boar crest on their tunics.

"What are you doing here?" Vark demands.

The first male gives us a broad smile, showing off his tusks, but it doesn't reach his eyes. "Just stretching our legs, friend."

"You are not my friend. And you can stretch your legs in your quarters—or outside. This is the king's corridor."

Vark's words are curt and angry, and I wonder at the change in his demeanor. He's the most laid-back warrior I've met so far, apart from Neekar, who is much younger than him. But now, he's every bit the fierce guard, and I wouldn't want to get on his bad side.

Apparently, the strangers recognize that, too. "Forgive us. We got lost."

As they walk past us, Vark and Steagor step in front of Mara and me, preventing the two males from brushing up against us. Still, the second orc leers at Mara in a way that has me shuddering in disgust.

"Who are they?" I whisper once they disappear around the bend.

Mara exchanges a look with Vark. "You should ask Gorvor about that. It's not our story to tell."

Vark nods in agreement, then frowns down at me. "My lady, would you mind returning to the great hall to wait for the king's return? I don't want to leave you with only one guard, but someone needs to inform the men stationed in the hall that they should keep an eye on those two."

"Of course," I say. "Whatever you need."

We all troop back down the corridor, Vark at the front and Steagor bringing up the rear. That they're genuinely concerned about my safety is touching—and more than a little worrying. Especially since Mara seems concerned as well, chewing on her lip as we walk.

Something strange is going on, and I intend to find out what it is. It might be difficult with the guards always following me around, but I'll start at the source.

I'll need to question the king.

EIGHT

Dinnertime comes and passes, and still the hunting party hasn't returned. The cook brings me a bowl of strawberries and a delicious yeasted cake to go with it, and I share my loot with Mara and my guards again. The king's cousin is easy to talk to, and she tells me that when she's not escorting me around, she's responsible for making sure everything in the settlement runs smoothly. She calls herself the steward, and having seen how large the Hill is, I understand the importance of her role.

"You don't have to keep me company tomorrow," I tell her. "I'll manage on my own now that you've shown me around. You must have a lot of work to do."

She relaxes on the bench, her elbows on the table. "You can come and help me. It wouldn't hurt for you to know how our people live."

I agree immediately, glad of the suggestion. If I'm going to stay here, I don't want to be a burden. If anything has stuck with me today, it's that everyone in the settlement has their role. No idle hands in the orc kingdom. And I don't want to be the exception, the lady who lounges in her bed all day or has guards escorting her as she strolls through the corridors while others work.

The only thing casting a pall over today is the presence of those four strange orcs, the ones no one wants to talk about. They sit at a table on the other side of the hall, talking in quiet voices, and even though orc hearing is excellent, it seems none of my companions can make out what they're saying because of the noise in the hall. The strangers have chosen their spot perfectly—they're in plain view, yet their conversation can remain private.

Suddenly, cheers sound from one of the other entrance tunnels to the great hall. I sit straight, wondering at the commotion, when a group of orcs stride into the chamber.

It takes me only a moment to single out Gorvor at the head of the hunting party. He's grinning, his scarred chest smudged with earth and something dark—*blood*. My heart beats faster in a worried flutter until I realize it's not his blood. No, the orc king is carrying a big, brown *something* slung across his shoulders.

He walks to the entrance to the kitchens, where the head cook and several of his helpers are waiting with sharpened knives. Gorvor heaves the animal carcass over his head without even breathing hard and deposits it on one of the tables.

It's a boar. A large adult boar, which must weigh as much as a human man, and yet the king handles it like it's a rabbit.

He faces us again, and the orcs in the hall cheer, the noise rising and echoing from the walls. Only the strange group of four remain seated, glowering at the king. And he smirks, his handsome face haughty and proud.

This is a message.

One by one, the other members of the hunting party

bring their kills to the kitchen table. It's a massive pile of animals, so their hunt must have been a great success. In the human world, a supply like this could feed a village for weeks. But I've seen how much each orc can eat, so I understand the need for this much food. That the king helps provide for his people is a significant gesture, too—and completely different from human lords who put unfair taxes on their people and live off their peasants' work.

Very deliberately, Gorvor turns his back on the strange orcs and strides toward us. I didn't think he'd seen us, but his dark gaze falls on me, and I know he's only been biding his time. In one leap, he's at my side. He wraps his hands around my waist, lifts me from my seat on the bench, and hauls me in for a kiss.

In front of *everyone*.

More cheers from the crowd, but I barely hear them. Gorvor kisses me deeply, his tongue invading my mouth. He smells so good, I want to crawl inside him. That scent of the forest and fire, combined with dirt and sweat he'd collected throughout the day, is tantalizing and addictive. I inhale deeply, realizing he's doing the same.

"You didn't wash me off," he says, sniffing at my temple.

I shake my head in answer, too busy trying to kiss him again. If he likes his scent on me, I'll take care to not bathe while he's gone. He supports my weight easily, but I wrap my legs around his waist and loop my arms around his neck. A small part of me is horrified at this public display, but I don't care. Not when he squeezes my thighs through my dress and grinds his hips up in a way that leaves very little to imagination.

"See you tomorrow, then?" Mara snickers, breaking the spell.

Gorvor growls at her, but when I peer up at his face, he's grinning, and I think she might be one of the few clan members who would dare tease the king like this. A blush warms my cheeks, but I don't let go. I'm perfectly content where I am.

Well, that's not true. I'm happy in Gorvor's arms, yes, but my need rises in my belly, warm embers fanned to flames with every slide of my body against his.

His nostrils flare as he inhales, and his gaze darkens. "Aye. We will see you tomorrow."

Without waiting for anyone's reply, he clutches me closer to his chest and marches from the great hall and into the corridor leading to his room. From the quiet footsteps following us, I know the guards are behind us somewhere, but they stay hidden in shadows, unobtrusive. Still, I'm glad when Gorvor pushes his way through the door and slams it shut.

Then he makes a move as if to set me on the bed, but I cling to him, unwilling to let go.

"I need to wash, little mate. I am not clean." He gently unwraps my arms from around his neck and lays me on the bedcovers. "I will be very quick."

I protest, but he's having none of it. Still, I can't bring myself to pout *too* much, not when he strips naked in front of me and gives me a nice view of his backside. Like the rest of him, it's muscled and taut, and his back... Well, his back is a testament to his hard work, honed to perfection by what I imagine must have been grueling battle exercises and hunting. The scars I'd seen on his chest and shoulders are visible here as well, silvery lines and spots from untold wounds.

I bite my lip to stop the questions from bubbling up. If I start, I'll never stop, and I want *him* first. His body. His thick, proud cock. I don't know how it'll work, exactly, but I've decided to trust Gorvor that this is possible. That *we* are possible. The glowing sensation inside me, the mating bond, shines brighter with my inner admission that this is right. This is where I'm supposed to be, in the orc king's bed.

He washes quickly, just as he'd promised, and returns to me, dripping with water. I want to lick every drop from his skin, but he rubs himself all over with a bath sheet, his heated gaze on me. He's hard already, and I know he has the same plans for tonight as I do.

Silence stretches between us as he drops the linen on the floor and takes the last two steps to the bed. He sits on the edge and wraps his warm hand around my ankle.

"I want to fuck you tonight," he rumbles, looking straight into my eyes.

Emotions swell inside me, a heady mixture of apprehension, lust, and curiosity. I give him a small nod, only a jerk of my head.

The king's gaze radiates approval, and he slides his hand higher up my calf, caressing me slowly. "I will make sure you're ready, Dawn," he promises. "But you need to trust me."

I swallow past a suddenly tight throat. "I do."

Now he reaches my knee, and I let out a small giggle because I'm ticklish there, on the soft underside of my thighs. Gorvor's lips twitch up, and he repeats the movement, watching me intently as if he wants to explore all my responses. So I relax against the pillows and let him learn my body. We learn together, because I've never had anyone kiss the pale flesh of my thighs, and I didn't know until now how much I enjoyed it. Once, I try to sit up and caress him, but he pins me to the bed with a stern glower that has excitement fluttering in my belly.

What would he do if I disobeyed?

He pushes up my skirts, taking the thin linen shift with them, and I spread my knees wide to give him access. This is what he did this morning, and I anticipate the pleasure that will follow.

But he stops just short of kissing my pussy and growls, his eyes closed and his brow furrowed.

"What's wrong?" I ask, lifting up on my elbows.

He presses his forehead to my thigh, and a shudder goes through him. "I need to go slow."

I sit up fully and run my hand over his thick hair, down the braid he hasn't yet unraveled. "You *are*. You're taking care of me."

He shakes his head, and the gesture has his stubble scratching over my sensitive skin. "I could hurt you. If you knew what I wanted to do to you, Dawn... You would run from me, screaming, and I'd never get my mate back."

I caress the pointed tip of his green ear. "Tell me."

He grips the covers with both hands, his massive fists bunching on either side of me. "I cannot. You are so small and fragile."

Something squeezes inside me, a sadness that he's being denied what he clearly craves because his mate is human. If I hadn't seen how he looks at me, if I hadn't experienced the pleasure he'd showered me with this morning, I might have run away from him in this moment. But he'd said I was his mate. Fated. Perfect. He'd said he was mine, and I intend to honor that.

"Gorvor." I say his name gently and wait until he peers up at me. "Tell me."

He rolls to his back with a groan and throws his arm

over his eyes. His cock, so thick and beautiful, juts up, the knot at the bottom already bulging.

"I want to thrust inside you immediately," he tells me in a rough, rumbling voice. "Fill you up and have you take my knot."

I reach to my back and tug loose the first of my laces. "I know this already."

He scoffs. "You think you do. But your human man rutted you for a minute, and it was over, aye? I would take you over and over until you screamed with pleasure and your tight pussy would be filled with my seed."

Struggling with the rest of my laces, I let heat wash over me. The words are rude, but... "I'm not hearing anything that would put me off so far."

When had our roles changed from me trying to escape him to him talking himself out of this? It must be the mating bond between us. I disliked not being consulted about it, yes, but now that I've felt it, I can't deny its power. The pull toward Gorvor is so strong, thinking about leaving him causes me physical pain. I could no more do it than sever off my arm.

If this is my fate, I will do the best I can to make it fit. Like I've done every day in my old life, I'll work and get through it.

Not that being mated to a magnificent warrior like Gorvor is a hardship.

I tug the dress over my head, the last few laces be damned. A ripping sound tells me I'll have to fix something later, but I don't care. I bunch the dress and dump it over the side of the bed, then do the same with my shift, until I'm completely naked and out of breath.

Gorvor is still lying on his back with his eyes closed, clearly tormented. "I want your lips wrapped around my cock and to see you take so much you choke," he growls. "Then I'd put you on your hands and knees and fuck you from behind so I could watch how your pretty pussy takes my knot. You'd be limp with pleasure, but I'd hold you up and pinch your nipples until you screamed and climaxed again and again."

I gasp, picturing it all in my mind. He fists his cock in one large palm and gives himself a hard jerk. My pussy clenches at the sight, throbbing in response to those fantasies. And I can no longer hold back.

Feeling brave and more than a little reckless, I climb over Gorvor and straddle his thick thighs. His body tenses at the skin-to-skin contact, and he finally draws his arm away from his face.

"Dawn?"

His voice is both incredulous and hopeful, and the longing shining from his dark eyes melts the last defenses around my heart.

I scoot down his legs to put myself in the right position and peek at him through my lashes. "You said you wanted me to wrap my mouth around you?"

His quick inhale tells me everything I need to know. But still, I love how low his voice gets when he rumbles, "I did."

Tentatively, I grasp his shaft and lean over it. "I'm not sure if I can do this right. I've never tried it before."

He reaches for me and buries his fingers in my hair. "Just suck me."

The command sends heat skittering through my veins. It's so simple, so primal.

Just suck me.

I lower my head and kiss the broad green cockhead lightly. It's slick with precum, and I lick my lips, wetting them and tasting Gorvor for the first time. The salty-sweet, warm taste blooms on my tongue, and I clench my legs instinctively. But I can't close my thighs—the king widens his knees, spreading me over him.

"That's it," he murmurs. "I can smell your pussy growing wet for me."

My eyelids flutter shut as I bring my lips to his cock again. This time, I open them and glide down, taking the whole head in my mouth. It's hot, and I run my tongue around it, getting used to it.

Gorvor's fingers tighten in my hair, and he hisses in a breath. "Good girl. Now take me deeper."

I relax my jaw and slide down his cock, taking as much as I can. Then I bob up, sucking in my cheeks. With both hands, I grip the knot, squeezing in time with my movements.

"Aah," the king groans, throwing his head back. "You don't need instructions. You feel so good, little mate."

The knowledge that I can bring him as much pleasure as he does to me is powerful. I quicken my rhythm, sliding up and down his cock until his hips are rocking up to meet my mouth on every turn. The trickle of his precum intensifies, and I swallow it all down, enjoying the way Gorvor jerks every time I do it.

Suddenly, he grips my chin and pulls me off him, and I find myself airborne for a second, his hands at my waist. He lifts me easily, and I squeak, searching for somewhere to put my hands.

"What are you doing?" I cry.

He yanks me closer to his face, and I brace my hands on the wall behind his head on instinct. It's a strange position, with my knees on either side of his head, and I've never felt so exposed. He can see *everything*, and I don't doubt that he can smell how slick I've grown from pleasuring him.

"I wasn't done," I protest, trying to wiggle my way back down his body.

But his palms land on my ass, holding me in place. "I want to fuck you, Dawn. I need you ready."

"I am," I protest, "just let me—*oh!*"

My words taper off on a cry as he shoves my thighs farther apart and fastens his mouth on my pussy. His hot tongue licks over my sensitive bud, and pleasure explodes inside me, hot and sudden. I melt over him, barely supporting myself on the wall, but Gorvor has me pinned in place, holding me where he wants me.

Then he spears his tongue into my pussy, licking up all my slickness, and growls. The sound is savage and reverberates through my body. I've never heard anything like it, but some base, primal part of me loves how it makes me feel. I'm at his mercy, and his only mission is to bring me to my finish.

He returns his tongue to my pearl, teasing it with hard, long strokes, and wedges his hand between my spread thighs. "I need to stretch you. You'll ride my hand, and then you'll ride my cock."

He presses first one finger inside my slick pussy, then another, and I cry out in shock. But I'm so wet now that I take him easily, and I bear down on his hand, wanting more contact. I'm so empty inside, and it feels so damn good to have those hot fingers pushing deep.

Gorvor adds another finger. "Pinch your nipples," he commands.

I cup my full, aching breast with one hand, keeping the other braced on the wall, and bring my fingers to my nipple. When I squeeze, the sensation travels through my body and straight to my core, as if an invisible line of pleasure connects both. The pressure builds inside me, an onslaught

ZOE ASHWOOD

of sensation from all the different parts of my body being stroked and filled and pinched and—

It starts slowly, a rush of heat that grows, expanding until I'm consumed, overwhelmed. I cry out, rocking my hips down to chase more of that feeling, and Gorvor laps up all my wetness, keeping up with me. Shaken, I put both hands on the wall to keep myself from collapsing, and whimper as he pulls his fingers from me.

"You taste so good when you come," he murmurs, dragging his tongue lazily through my folds. "I could eat your pussy all day."

I laugh, shaken. "You will get no complaints from me."

Gorvor grins and drags his palm over his mouth, wiping away traces of me. Then he grabs my hips and moves me lower down his body, and I end up stretched on top of him, my chest pressed up against his. He's so warm, and the rapid beat of his heart echoes mine perfectly.

I should be sated, tired and spent, but the tension in Gorvor's muscles has me on edge. I want to know what more he has to show me. Everything up to this point has been exquisite, and I'm eager to learn.

The king keeps his gaze on mine as he urges me to sit up over his cock. Anticipation and a twinge of fear war in my head, but I want this. I do.

I'm not certain how we'll fit. Because even three of his fingers aren't nearly as large as the shaft currently notched at my pussy. It's long, yes, but more importantly, it's thick, and there's a part of me that balks at it, panicking.

I bite my lip and look between my legs. "You're just so *large*."

He chuckles deeply. "I am. But we were brought together, and you are my mate. This will work."

84

I brace my hands on his muscled chest and dig my fingers into his skin. "All right. But slowly."

He jerks his head in a nod, but the strain in his neck tells me this is costing him. He's suffering, sweat breaking out on his brow. His chest rises and falls with rapid breaths, but he doesn't force me, doesn't pull me down on his cock.

It's this restraint, the barely leashed power, that gives me courage. I spread my knees wider and reach between us to align us just right. Then I let my weight do the work as I bear down on the broad, warm cockhead.

It's big. I inhale through my nose and let the air out through my mouth. "Gorvor..."

I don't know what I'm asking for, only that my brain and my body are at odds, one telling me that this is impossible and the other urging me on because I'm aching and ready.

The king slides his hands up my thighs, past my belly, to cup both my breasts. The sight of his big green palms on me has my heart beating faster, and when he pinches my nipples, hard, I loosen over him.

The head of his cock slips inside me, and I groan, closing my eyes at the stretching sensation. It fills me up, the tip nudging at that wonderful place Gorvor showed me yesterday.

"This feels... Oh, it feels so good."

My voice comes out as a breathy, needy moan. At the same time, I'm aware I've barely taken the head of the king's cock, and I'm far from being done.

"Dawn," he groans. "You're beautiful. I never thought I'd find my mate, and there you were. So fucking perfect."

His words fall from his lips in a rush, as if he's been keeping them hidden and now they've been revealed. I don't want anything more between us—no pretense, no secrets.

"Help me," I gasp. "I need *more*."

His brow furrowed, he reaches between my legs and swirls his fingertips around my bud, and I slip an inch lower on his cock. We both shout out, and the shock of the rude intrusion has me clenching down on him, hard.

"You need to relax, little mate," Gorvor forces out through gritted teeth. "Or I might not last much longer."

That he's suffering, too, actually helps me. I can't help but laugh at our predicament. We're both in pain, though for different reasons.

"I'm sorry." I snort and cover my mouth with my hand. "This is too ridiculous."

I slide lower on a gasp, my body stretching to accommodate his. Gorvor gives me a grin in return, flashing his tusks, and caresses my pearl in slow, sensual circles.

"This is better." I rock forward a little. "I think it might work."

The wet slide of him through my pussy has me moaning, and I repeat the motion, each time taking a little bit more of his cock. Glancing down between us, at the green shaft impaling me, I groan and close my eyes, though. I haven't even reached his knot—and I have no idea how I'll take in *that* as well.

And if I can't, does that mean Gorvor and I aren't meant to be mated? Maybe the gods have made a mistake, and we're not compatible. Maybe he was never supposed to fit inside me.

The thought makes me unbearably sad—and that bond between us tightens, throbbing painfully.

"Shh." He brushes my hair away from my face. "Don't worry. There is no need to hurry."

He pushes himself up to a seated position, bringing his chest flush with mine. The angle between us changes, and I slip a tiny fraction lower, my thighs stretched wide. He kisses me, exploring my mouth with his tongue, thrusting in with the same slow, steady rhythm as he rocks me in his lap. With a bit of maneuvering, he has me loop my legs around his waist, and finally, finally, we are joined fully— apart from his knot.

The fullness is incredible. Every hard inch of his cock is buried inside me, and I instinctively squeeze my inner muscles around him. His knot presses up against my pussy, teasing me from the outside. Gorvor groans through our kiss and bites down on my lower lip. The sting of pain is fleeting, replaced by exquisite pleasure, and I kiss him back with everything I have.

"Dawn," he rumbles. "I need to come. Inside you. Right now."

His words are rough, each one punctuated by a harsh breath. The tension in his muscles is testament to how much this is costing him.

"Yes," I breathe against his lips. I'm ready. I can take it.

He buries his face in my shoulder and lets out a shuddering exhale. Then his fingers squeeze my hips, and he pulls me almost all the way off his cock and slides me back down in one long, forceful thrust. I'm wet enough now for his cock to glide smoothly, and we both groan, clinging to each other. He picks up the pace, and I ride him as best I can. I wrap my legs tight around his waist and undulate my hips in time with his thrusts. Gorvor gives me a feral, breathless grin, then kisses me roughly, taking full advantage.

My climax hits without warning. The thick shaft drags over my inner walls so well, and with a fierce thrust, Gorvor

ZOE ASHWOOD

sends me over the edge. I scream, all the sensations coalescing into one perfect, endless explosion of bliss. The coarse hair on his chest drags over my nipples, his tongue invades my mouth, and it's all too much, too good, too—

"Gods!" I bear down on his cock, needing more, even though I'm so full already. "Please, please!"

The king grips my waist, and with one last push, he slips his knot inside me. I gasp, clutching his shoulders. My fingernails dig into his warm skin, but he doesn't seem to care—he kisses me deeply, then tears his mouth away from mine and bellows, coming hard. A rush of warmth floods my pussy, his cum coating his cock and slicking me up so we slide together so perfectly.

The hot, bulging knot pulses inside me, triggering another climax in me. I cry out in shock and delight—the throbbing pressure against my inner walls feels like nothing I've imagined, and it's almost unbearably good. I squeeze my eyes shut, overwhelmed.

A big hand closes around my chin.

"Look at me, Dawn," the king growls. "Look at me when you come."

I force my lids open and stare into Gorvor's dark eyes, so feral, focused all on me. He holds my hip with one hand and digs the fingers of his other hand into my hair, bringing me closer for another scorching kiss.

"You took my knot." His breath mingles with mine as our foreheads touch. "Little mate, you're incredible. I can feel your sweet pussy squeezing me."

I shift in his lap, trying to see if we're really locked together like he said we would be, and we both shout at the sensation. It's so intense, another flutter of pleasure pulses in my core.

"How—how long will we stay like this?" I tighten my

88

legs around his waist in an effort to stay still. I don't know if I can take another round of such exquisite torture.

He frowns down at me. "You don't like it?"

"No, I do," I answer truthfully. "But it's so..."

I try to find the right words to describe what I'm feeling. With our bodies locked together, naked, I'm so exposed. I've never been this close to someone, and I don't just mean that in a sexual way. There's no hiding from Gorvor's piercing gaze, not here.

He strokes his palm over my back, a slow, soothing caress. "What is it?"

Taking a deep breath, I say, "It's very...intimate. More than I imagined it would be."

His palm makes circles on my skin, hypnotic. "What did you imagine?"

I can't look him in the eyes anymore, so I drop my gaze to his chest. "I didn't think you'd be so good to me."

His scowl darkens, and I hurry on to explain before he jumps to the wrong conclusions.

"I didn't think you'd hurt me. Well, not after the first, um, visit to this room," I say. "You kept your word and you showed me *pleasure*. That was incredible."

He flashes me a smug smile, and I smack his shoulder lightly. He laughs, but still, he rubs my back as if he's trying to keep me talking. All the while, I'm so, so aware of the rigid length buried inside me. It hasn't softened one bit, and the sensations it brings out in me are no less intense than before. It's a strange sensation, to be talking when we're...connected.

"I didn't think there would be a real place for me in your life," I conclude. "I'm human. You're an orc."

"And that's bad?" he asks. "Did you want a human mate? A husband?"

I bite my lip, wondering how to explain. "I never expected to marry."

He moves beneath me to lean back against the headboard, and the knot triggers another wave of intense heat in my pussy. It's not enough to push me into a climax, but I gasp and cling to his shoulders, waiting for him to settle.

"You are a beautiful young woman," he grumbles. "Are human men so blind that they didn't see that?"

His words warm my heart, but there's so much more than that involved in a human relationship. The next part is hard for me to admit, though, so I duck my chin and decide to just get it over with quickly.

"First of all, I wasn't considered exceptionally pretty among humans," I mutter. "If I had been, things might have been easier. But to top that, I had no money—and no family."

He takes my chin again and lifts my face. I still don't want to look at him, but he doesn't make me. He drops a kiss on my lips, his tusks touching my cheeks lightly.

"I am sorry you lost your family," he says. "But you are here now. You have a new family."

Tears prick behind my eyelids, and I don't want to cry now. I also don't want to explain how wrong he is. I haven't lost my family. My parents just didn't want me. So I wrap myself around him and squeeze, showing him with my body what I can't say with words.

"Ah, Dawn!" His big body jerks upright. "Gods, woman."

I giggle despite myself, realizing I must have squeezed *all* my muscles, even the inner ones. His hands land on my hips, and he pushes me down slightly, at the same time rocking up his hips as if he can't help himself. The knot jerks inside me, and I feel an answering pulse of his cum as he unloads himself again.

I scream his name, pleasure overtaking me, and moments later, slump limp against his chest, already so spent.

"I didn't know you could come more than once," I croak between panting breaths. "What else can you do?"

He chuckles, the sound reverberating in his broad chest. "Do you like it, Dawn? Having a big orc mate who can fill you up with his seed over and over in a single night?"

I bite my lip, then nod—just once, because it's difficult to admit, especially since I'm also worried about getting pregnant. But nothing has ever felt better than having Gorvor deep inside, telling me all these outrageous, beautiful things that make me hope for a better future.

"Good," he replies. "Then hold on."

CHAPTER
NINE

Gorvor coaxes another screaming climax from me before coming deep inside me. Then he carries me to the bathing pool where we cuddle and kiss until his knot finally subsides and I can slip off him. We wash each other, reluctant to leave the warm embrace of the water. But I'm dead tired, so he bundles me up in a blanket and carries me back to bed, where he shifts me to the side and fits his hot, muscular body behind me.

I don't complain—in fact, I sleep soundly and without nightmares again. And when I wake, the king is right there with me.

"Good morning," he rumbles and rolls on his back.

He grabs my hips and lifts me on top of his chest, so I put my hands beneath my chin and get comfortable on my stomach, looking down at him.

I take a deep inhale, closing my eyes in bliss. "How is it that you smell so nice? I've only seen you use the same soap I've been using, and that's not the scent I'm getting."

He palms the backs of my thighs and caresses the soft skin there. "What do I smell like to you?"

I wiggle higher and put my nose right up to his neck. "Like I'm standing in the middle of the forest. With damp earth and fresh tree scents. But also of fire. Of a warm, cozy fire. It reminds me of—"

Biting my tongue, I stop myself and press my cheek against his shoulder, trying to hide my blush. I was going to say it reminds me of home, which is strange, because the only home I ever remember having definitely never smelled like that.

"Tell me," he commands.

I swallow past a suddenly tight throat. "You smell like home."

His hands still on my ass, and I get the feeling he doesn't even know he's doing it. Orcs are so much more used to touching each other that his caresses aren't really sexual, not now.

He hums deep in his chest. "To me, you smell of freshly baked honey cakes. The kind the cook only ever makes on my name day. And of sweet summer flowers." He lets out a huff. "Every breath I take is a celebration."

Tears fill my eyes, and no matter how much I blink, I can't stop them from falling. When I sniffle and try to hide it, Gorvor lifts his head and looks down at me.

"Ah, little mate," he says, sounding dismayed. "What did we say about crying?"

"No tears," I hiccup. "I'm sorry. I'll stop."

Only I don't. I cry harder, the emotions pouring out in a rush. Without a tissue to hide behind, I cover my face with my hands and try to slip away from Gorvor to keep him from witnessing my blubbering.

But he gently sets me on the bed by his side and pries my hands away from my eyes. He kisses away my tears and dabs at my face with the corner of the bedsheet, clumsy but earnest. And suddenly, I understand—he doesn't hate crying, he just has no idea how to deal with me when I'm sad.

"Will you hold me?" I croak. "That will help me the most."

Immediately, he wraps his big arms around me and tucks me against his chest. Under the wool covers, our cocoon is almost unbearably warm, but I wouldn't leave it for the world. My sobbing subsides, and I hiccup, then wipe my tears and press a kiss in the center of Gorvor's chest.

"Thank you," I whisper.

A long, long time has passed since anyone held me when I was upset. I can't even remember the occasion, and that brings fresh pain to my heart, because I haven't let myself admit that I craved it. So much.

And now that I'm here, in the king's bed, in his arms, I'm afraid of what it might do to me if he ever decides he doesn't want me after all. To taste this closeness—not only the pleasure of sex but this intimate embrace, offering comfort—is wonderful, but losing it would rip me apart. Everything has happened so fast, with Gorvor insisting I'm his mate, but I don't even know what it means, not really.

I want to spend the whole day here, pretending my past doesn't exist, but my body demands I take care of it. I'm sore from our...fucking last night. The hot water helped, but as much as I wish to get Gorvor's cock inside me again, I think giving myself some rest would be a good idea.

"Are you hurt?" he asks when he notices my wince as I get up from bed to use the privy.

"No," I say quickly, but at his doubting look, I amend, "Not much. Just a little tender."

His brows furrow, and he hunches his broad shoulders. "I didn't want that. I was too rough with you."

I return to his side and palm his face with both hands. "No. You were perfect. And I love how big you are. You filled me up so good. And it felt *amazing*."

He grips my waist, but I dance away from him.

"I do need to use the bathroom first," I tell him, blushing. "Then I'll be ready for more."

But when I duck behind the tapestry to relieve myself, the slide of the bolts and the door opening and closing send a jolt through me. After I'm done, I dart back out—and find the room empty.

Gorvor has left.

The pang of disappointment takes me by surprise. I was sure he was going to demand more, maybe even take the morning off to spend it in bed with me.

I wash and dress in fresh clothes that someone has brought for me. Orcs seem intent on cleanliness, which makes sense considering their much more sensitive noses, so I take care of myself as well, not wanting to be known as the filthy human. I'm different enough as it is, and all I want to do is blend in and make myself less conspicuous.

I don't know why I expected more from the king. He must have important duties to take care of, much more pressing than attending to his mate's whims. Still, my good mood sours.

I'm braiding my hair when the door swings open and Gorvor strides in, shirtless and looking too good to be allowed.

When have I stopped thinking about him as a brute and started being so damn attracted to him? The breadth of his shoulders no longer intimidates me, and the scars on his skin only spur my curiosity. His tusks don't seem so scary anymore, either. I want to dig my fingers into his long black hair and press myself to his muscled chest.

He frowns as he sets his gaze on me. "Are you going somewhere?"

My mouth is full of hairpins, so I remain silent for a minute and finish sticking them into my braided crown. Then I look up at him from my perch on the bed. "I thought you'd left."

I don't want to sound whiny and petulant, yet I can't help but pout a little. What else was I supposed to think?

Gorvor walks to the bed, towering over me. He bends down and runs his thumb over my lower lip, something like amusement and affection lighting up his dark eyes. Up close, I notice his black eyelashes and the warm, earthy browns of his irises. My heart stutters, and warmth coils in my belly at his attention.

"Don't worry, Dawn," he rumbles. "I'm here."

Then he kisses me, his rough tongue invading my mouth, seducing me slowly with each thorough lick. I'm panting by the time he pulls back and wordlessly offers me a cloth bag with something bulky in it.

I take it, curiosity getting the better of me. It makes a clinking sound, and when I open the top, I find three jars inside.

Handling them with care, I place them on the messy covers. "What are these?"

Gorvor sits next to me and taps the first jar, filled with crushed herbs. "This is the fertility tea. The herbalist insisted I take it when I came asking for this." He points to a small pot of greenish goop.

"And what is this?" I ask, looking up at him.

His lips twist in a wicked smile. "A salve. For your pussy."

Heat slams into my cheeks, and I jerk my hand back from where I was reaching for the pot. "What?"

"You said you were sore," he explains, "so I got you something to soothe the pain and help you heal."

"Oh." I cover my face with my hands, mortified and touched at once. "Thank you."

He tugs my hands away and gives me another devastating kiss. Then he breaks the connection and motions at the third jar. "That one is different."

I raise my eyebrows at him. He shifts closer to me and lifts me into his lap. Instinctively, I wrap my arms around his neck, and his big palms land on my ass, pulling me closer. The hard ridge of his erection presses against my thigh, letting me know how much he wants me.

"It's a tea to keep you from getting pregnant," he murmurs. "She almost didn't want to give it to me, but I insisted."

I stare wordlessly up at him. That he would get me such a thing...

Gorvor's smile tugs up on one side. "Everyone is keen for their king to produce many heirs. Fat little babies, ready to learn all they can." He brushes his fingers over my cheek and tucks my hair behind my ear. "But I know you might not be ready. I hope you will not drink this tea but I want you to have the choice."

His expression seems pained, as if it's physically hurting him to admit this. My heart swells, and I bury my face in his neck, overwhelmed.

"Thank you," I whisper. "For thinking of me."

Nobody has ever put me and my wishes first. Not my parents, not the innkeeper I worked for, and certainly none of the men I'd had the displeasure to meet. But this huge orc... He understands me better than anyone.

I loosen my grip on him and peer up through my eyelashes. "Will you..."

I want to say the words, but they won't leave my lips. It's too scandalous, even after everything we've done together.

He takes my chin and lifts it. "What is it?"

Oh, why not?

"Will you help me apply the salve?" I blurt, flushing all over my skin.

He hums, and his grip on my waist tightens. "Is that what you want? For me to take care of your pussy?"

I nod, breathless. "Please."

He tosses me on the bed with one effortless push, and I land on the pillows, giggling. His eyes glitter with heat as he picks up the small pot.

"Lie back," he commands. "And close your eyes."

I start to protest—I want to see whatever he'll do to me —but he taps my ankle impatiently, waiting for me to obey. Huffing, I lean back and close my eyes.

Instantly, all my other senses intensify, and I experience every touch, every scent as if it's magnified. Gorvor slides his palms up my calves, pushing up the skirts of my dress. Then he guides my knees apart, and I gasp at what I imagine I must look like, bared to him completely.

He leans in, and his hot breath on my sex is the only warning I get before he spreads me with his fingers and licks a long line over my pussy. I cry out, trying to close my legs, but he's there, wedged rudely between my thighs.

"Shh," he says. "Let me do this for you."

He licks my pearl, teasing it with flicks of his tongue, then pushing me higher with long, luxurious laps. I plead to have his fingers, too, or his cock, but he doesn't give me what I want.

"Later," he promises between sucking my bud. "I will fill you up, and you will take it, but first, you need to heal."

He brings me to a climax, coaxing it out of me in an embarrassingly short time. At this point, I don't have to force myself to close my eyes—I'm spent and happy to lie back and let him do all the work.

The fresh scent of herbs invades my nose, and I realize he must have uncapped the salve. The first touch of his fingers to my oversensitive pussy has me jerking in surprise. The salve is cool against my hot flesh, and it tingles slightly. Whatever is in it is more potent than just the herbs I scent—I've heard whispers of mages still hiding in the forests of Bellhaven, but I'd thought that was just a rumor.

Maybe *some* of the stories circulating through taprooms in the human world are true after all.

Gorvor teases my pussy, then gentles me with a hand to my belly and spreads the ointment all over my tender flesh. He pushes one long finger inside me, and I swear he hooks it up at just the right spot, drawing a gasp from me.

"You're an evil orc," I complain, finally peeking at him. "You'll leave me as needy as I was before this."

He chuckles. "And I will be uncomfortable all day with a hard cock, thinking of your tight little sheath."

I bite my lip, an idea forming in my mind. I wait for him to finish his task. He smooths my skirts back down and gives an almighty sigh.

"I must return to my duties," he rumbles. "Even if I wish we could remain here for days, fucking and sleeping."

I sit up and take his hand. "But can your duties wait a while longer?"

He smiles, and for the first time, I notice a slight dimple in his cheek, beneath the black stubble. "What did you have in mind?"

A shiver runs through my body, but I make myself say

the words out loud. "Will you let me...lick you? Like you did with me just now?"

TEN

Gorvor lets out a rough exhale. "Aye."

"Show me how?"

He grips my fingers tight and stands, pulling me with him. He guides me onto one of the soft furs that line the earthen floor like carpets. "Now go to your knees."

I obey, sinking to the fur in front of him. The position makes it clear how Gorvor wants me to pleasure him. I reach for the laces of his leather pants and tug.

"That's it. Take out my cock." His voice is rough and low, betraying his emotion.

I spread the leather flaps and ease them down, freeing the king's erection. It's hard, the knot bulging at the bottom. The shaft itself is green and ridged with veins, but the skin covering it is velvet-smooth and warm. Below his knot, his balls are pulled tight already, large and half hidden in coarse black hair.

I reach down first and cup them, running my fingers all over, exploring what he likes. Gorvor remains quiet and stoic until I grip his balls firmly and give them a light tug.

Then his hips rock forward, and his cock kicks in front of me, leaking precum.

"Don't tease," he rumbles. "Unless you want me to—*ah!*"

His words dissolve on a hoarse cry when I wrap my lips around his green cockhead. It's large, and I breathe through my nose, adjusting to his size. Like last night, I can't take all of him, but I do my best, sliding up and down his shaft, sucking as I go.

His composure cracks, and he grips the back of my neck, his fingers digging into my scalp. He shows me how fast he wants me to go, and soon, his hips are rocking with the movements, his breaths sawing in and out of his big chest.

"Dawn," he groans. "I want you to touch yourself."

I glance up, mouth full.

His dark eyes glitter with intent. "Get yourself wet. Because when I come in your pretty little mouth, I'll want to fuck you, too."

Heat rushes through my limbs and gathers low in my belly. I release Gorvor's leg, where I'd been bracing one hand, and ruck up my skirts until I can reach the apex of my thighs. I'm wet, slick from both my own desire and the salve he rubbed all over me earlier. It has taken away the sting, the ache left by our lovemaking last night. I swipe my fingertips over my pearl, and I moan around Gorvor's cock, my hips jerking.

He fills my ears with filthy promises, and I work his cock as my legs tremble. I'm close to my climax, and the king still hasn't finished.

This won't do.

On my next retreat, I suck my cheeks in, then increase my speed. He showed me what he liked, but not what would make him fall apart. I'll have to figure that out on my own. He hisses a breath through his teeth as I wrap my fingers around his knot as far as they will go and give him a strong squeeze. His grip tightens in my hair, and I know I'm on the right track.

Then I hum around his cock, and he roars, his head thrown back, the green tendons in his neck standing out. He thrusts his hips forward, and he's coming, powerful jets of cum shooting into my mouth and down my throat. I swallow, but there's a lot, and I let his cock slip from my lips, spilling his seed on my chest. We're making a mess, but I don't care because it feels *amazing* to see him let go and lose control.

I pull my hand from under my skirt and brace myself. The king draws in a huge breath, his nostrils flaring, and then he's on me. He drops to his knees, grabs me by my waist, and flips me around. I land on my hands and knees, panting, and gaze over my shoulder at him. With his cock still out and hard, he looks magnificent, and he's staring at me like he wants to devour me.

"I need you," he growls. "Are you wet for me, Dawn?"

"Yes!" I rock my hips back. "So wet."

He flips my skirts up, exposing my skin, and groans at the sight of me. I spread my knees to get more leverage. His palms land on my ass, and he kneads my flesh, then runs his blunt fingers down my crack to my dripping pussy. He shoves in two fingers at once, making sure I'm ready.

"Please, please," I beg, riding his hand. "I need to come."

He removes his hand and fits himself behind me. Then he takes my waist with both hands and pulls me back, impaling me on his thick cock. I scream in pleasure, chanting his name over and over as he drives himself in all the way to his knot.

Slowly, he withdraws. "I cannot go easy on you," he rasps. "Not today."

I lower myself to my elbows and duck my head. "Then don't."

Gorvor roars and plunges inside me, slamming his cock deep. His thighs meet mine, and the coarse hair dragging over my heated skin adds another layer of stimulation. Again, he retreats almost all the way and pushes in, and the slide of his veined shaft over my inner walls is enough to have me moaning.

Then his massive palm lands on my back, and he pushes me down, until my face is pressed into the soft fur and my hips jut up. The move changes the angle between us. His cock fills me, and I whimper, starbursts of pleasure exploding behind my closed eyelids.

"Put your fingers to your pussy," he commands, his words slurring with pleasure. "Feel how I fuck you."

His order is impossible to disobey. I wedge my hand under my body and reach between my legs, where he powers into me with increasing speed. His skin slaps against mine, but it's the feeling of his slick cock sliding into my pussy that has my legs trembling with tension. Then I reach for the sensitive button at the top of my slit and press down hard.

Gorvor slams inside me, his big body curling over mine. "Come for me, Dawn."

He fucks me deep, and I shatter, my mouth opening on a silent scream. On the next pulse of his cock, the knot slips inside me as if my body was made to take it at this exact moment of bliss. He fills me completely, and he bellows his release, shooting hot jets of cum. His thrusts grow shallower as we lock together, prolonging my pleasure.

I turn my face to the side, the fur sliding over my cheek

in stark contrast with the rough treatment I just got. I loved both—and especially the way Gorvor seems to know my body and exactly what I need.

"Was I too rough?" he asks quietly.

I shake my head and force myself to lift on shaking arms. "No. I loved it."

He caresses my back and slips his fingers to my scalp, where he massages away any tension, leaving me a soft, tired mess. Then he gathers me in his arms, my dress rustling all around us, and carries me to the bed, where he sits against the headboard with me spread over his lap. He rains soft kisses over my neck and shoulders and draws the pins from my ruined braid, all the while pulsing inside me.

And for once, I allow myself to relax completely. This isn't some quick rutting where we would both be more than eager to escape each other's company after it was done. No, Gorvor wraps his arms around me and gazes at me like I'm the sun and the moon, all in one disheveled human package.

When his knot releases, we wash again—and I'm beginning to understand why orcs are so keen on bathing. My dress is sticky with the remains of our pleasure, and Gorvor uses it to mop up the worst of the mess, then tosses it in a hamper by the door.

At my mortified look, he laughs and says, "Don't worry, this will be no surprise to the laundry folk. Orcs fuck a lot. At last, the king is doing it, too."

I press my hand over my mouth but can't stifle a giggle. "You're horrible."

He smacks my bare ass. "And you're a temptress. Now get dressed before I drag you back to bed. We both have work to do today."

I am almost tempted to sway my hips and bend over on

purpose to see what he'll do, but he's right. I promised Mara I'd help her, and we've already wasted half the morning in bed. Not that I count what we did a waste.

I go to pick a clean shift, and my gaze falls on the two jars of tea, clearly labeled to avoid confusion. One to promote a pregnancy, the other to prevent it. I collect both and set them at the bottom of the chest Gorvor designated for my use. It's the wrong time of month for me to worry about this, and I don't have to make the decision yet.

I don't immediately reach for the pregnancy preventing tea, and that's telling in and of itself. I would have thought this would be the only choice for me—drinking the tea and making sure I don't get pregnant. But something stops me. If my future is here, with the king, might I consider creating a family of my own? Would I have the support needed to raise a baby—and one not entirely human to boot?

I close the chest and put the matter from my mind.

For now.

For now, I can pretend and enjoy this as if tomorrow doesn't matter.

ELEVEN

I work with Mara through the next several days. The orc settlement is large and requires careful management to keep everything running smoothly, and the king's cousin oversees it all with an eagle eye for detail. We visit every part of the underground village, and Mara stops to introduce me to everyone we meet. The orcs are kind but wary, which is understandable—but not one of them treats me with disrespect or judgment.

I try to imagine what would happen if Mara came to live in my old human village, and cringe. Humans would be much less welcoming to an orc than orcs are of me, and I'm more and more ashamed of my earlier prejudice about their race.

She explains that her role—that of the steward—would generally fall to me, as the queen, but I assure her that I have no intention of taking it from her unless she wants to do something else. We agree that she would be my teacher for as long as necessary, which is a relief. I am in no way equipped for running an operation of this magnitude yet.

I don't often see the king during the day. His duties

center around protecting the Hill from outsiders, both orcs and humans, who might covet what he has built here for his people. He also takes care of trading with the neighboring towns, such as Ultrup, where I'd been bought at auction, and hunting to provide for the many hungry mouths that live here. In the kitchens, Mara explains how they are already preparing food for the long winter months, storing casks of salted meat and preserved produce in cold cellars to last through the infertile part of the year.

Everyone in the anthill-like village has a role, and though orcs love to celebrate and enjoy themselves in the evenings, they're hard workers. I do my best to follow their example, and I drag myself back to our room every night, exhausted but happy.

Yet I'm never too tired for Gorvor. We find each other in the dark, joining in slow, languid strokes or quickly, with mingling breaths, until we shatter in mutual pleasure.

One night, after our lovemaking and a bath that led to more petting and stroking, I lie naked on top of Gorvor's chest, idly drawing patterns on his still-damp skin. His eyes are closed, his breaths even and deep, and this might not be the best time to start an uncomfortable conversation, but I can no longer hold back my questions.

"Gorvor?" I poke him lightly in his rock-hard chest.

"Hmm?" He cracks one eye open and peers at me.

I shuffle off him and draw my legs in, looking down at his face. "Listen, I've been meaning to ask you something, but there's never been a good opportunity."

He lifts himself on his elbows. "Anything you want, you can ask."

My heart warms at the words. He means it. He really does. So why am I so nervous talking about this?

"I wanted to ask you about the four orcs who wear the

boar emblem," I say. "I've seen them around, and they always seem to be alone."

The king's expression shutters, and he sits up fully, creating a gap between us. I shiver, missing his heat instantly. He remains silent, though, so I soldier on.

"It's just that Vark and Steagor seem so suspicious of them," I press. "And when the other guards, Neekar and Ozork, saw them, Ozork had to haul Neekar away to stop him from jumping on them. And Mara won't talk about what's going on."

"I should hope not," Gorvor barks. "It's not her place."

I push my hair back, worry and frustration warring inside me. "But I don't *understand*. Are they your enemies? Then why are they here? They don't seem to *do* anything, they just lurk around and pop up at strange moments."

Just yesterday, I caught their leader staring at me intently from the other side of the great hall when I was helping Mara. He'd looked away, but I couldn't shake the feeling that his intentions weren't good.

"That doesn't concern you," he answers, scowling. "You only need to make sure you stay away from the Boar Clan orcs. I thought Vark and Steagor understood their orders, but maybe I need to change your guard. Or assign more warriors to you if they're unable to keep them away from you."

The Boar Clan orcs. At least I can put a name to them, sort of.

"There's no need for that." I gather the sheets around me, suddenly feeling very naked. I've never heard him speak so harshly to me, in such a cold voice. "It wasn't their fault, and I didn't even talk to those orcs. Please, I don't want to get the guards in trouble. Vark and Steagor did everything right. I was never in any danger."

Gorvor's chest heaves with a deep breath. "Still, I will talk to them."

"And you won't tell me anything?" I ask, dismayed. "I don't even know why I must avoid them."

"No," he snaps. "And your king's order should be enough for you to obey it."

I draw back, stung. He's never used his position to bully me into anything before.

"All right, my lord," I reply quietly. "I shall obey."

I slip from the bed and walk over to my chest. Every night since I've become Gorvor's mate, I've slept naked beside him, and loved it. But tonight, I feel like I need a shield between us, so I pull on a simple shift and tie it around my waist.

"Dawn." My name falls from his lips on a long exhale.

I stiffen but don't reply. He hurt me, and I won't be so easily swayed. Walking to the lantern hanging by the door, placed there for my benefit, I blow out its flame and make my careful way back to bed in the dark. I perch on the end of the bed, fluff my pillow, and lie as far away from Gorvor as possible, facing away from him.

The bed dips behind me, and strong arms wrap around my body. He tugs me into the center of the bed, against his chest. He buries his face in my hair. "I'm sorry."

I wait for an explanation, for something more, but it doesn't come. He's sorry for the way he treated me but not for keeping the truth from me.

Inside me, two impulses are at war, one demanding that I should ferret out his secrets by any means possible, the other insisting that Gorvor is a *king*, therefore entitled to keep things from me if he so chooses.

Am I stupid for trusting a man who does not trust me in turn?

Have you told him all your deepest secrets, then?

Guilt washes over me, and I roll into his embrace, settling down to sleep. Gorvor presses a kiss on top of my head and soon dozes off, his heartbeat slowing.

But I lie awake for a long time, trying to figure out how to go on.

TWELVE

I get my courses the next morning and learn of another peculiarity of the orc society. When I wake up and find a spot of blood on my shift and another on the linen sheet beneath me, I flush deeply and try to pull it from underneath Gorvor's bulky body so I can wash it and remove the stain before he notices it.

He wakes before I can execute my stealthy plan, though, takes one look at the blood, and springs into action. Apparently, women who have their courses are to be pampered and taken care of. He sends a servant running for fresh sheets, then carries me to the large bathing tub and sets me in the water, asking whether I need anything.

I try to explain to him that I'm fine and only need some linen strips to take care of things, but he insists I stay in bed all day. The servant returns not only with a change of bedding but also with a small wicker basket filled with soft undergarments designed to catch the women's monthly blood. I've never seen anything alike, and it's a genius idea.

"We should sew more of these and sell them at the human market," I declare after I wrap myself in a bath sheet and dry my skin. "Human women of all ages will fight for them, I can tell you that."

Gorvor chuckles as he tucks me into the freshly made bed. "That can be your first personal contribution to the clan. You can ask Mara to assign you a seamstress or two. I'm sure you'll find a way."

Pleasure glows inside me at his acceptance. Any other man would dismiss the idea as silly because it's meant specifically for women, but not this orc. He's thoughtful and kind, and I shouldn't care that he's keeping secrets from me. In time, he might trust me more.

Will I be happy if he never confides in me? If after a year or a decade together, he still demands my obedience without explanation? I don't know. It's a question I cannot answer yet. I will have to wait and see.

But maybe I could start by letting him know some of my past. I smooth the fresh sheet over my lap and force myself to speak.

"You know," I begin, "I was thirteen the first time I got my courses."

Gorvor sits on the bed next to me and raises his eyebrows. "That's early. Orc maidens don't get them until they're seventeen or so."

"Lucky them." I smile, though it's hard with the memories swirling through my mind. "It was on that day that my parents signed a contract with their neighbor to sell me to him as a wife."

He stiffens at my side. "What?"

I gaze at the ceiling because meeting Gorvor's gaze is too hard. "Indeed. We were poor, and he had the money to take me off my parents' hands. They would have gotten a nice sum for me."

I know exactly what they thought I was worth. Three

gold marks, a pair of good laying chickens, and a bag of turnips.

It's the turnips that still hurts to this day.

"But you were a child," Gorvor exclaims. He seems angry on my behalf, which soothes some of my old pain.

I shrug. "I bled, so I could be bedded."

His green skin goes ashen, and he clasps my hand. "That's barbaric. And humans say orcs are the evil ones."

I offer him a wry smile. "Anything that's different, we hate. Even I was different, and I look exactly like them. But my unwillingness to marry, to submit to some unwashed man more than three times my age, made me a freak."

He frowns fiercely and presses our joined hands to his heart. "You never need to worry again, little mate. I'll protect you. From humans. From orcs. From anyone who would wish to hurt you."

His words soothe me and allow me to continue. "I begged my parents not to make me go. To let me wait another winter, at least. I don't know if an additional year might have changed anything, but I think at that point, I was hoping for a miracle."

"I wish I'd been there to protect you." He gathers me in his arms and tucks my head beneath his chin.

I laugh. "I would pay good money to see that. A young, handsome orc, barging into my parents' house and dragging me off to safety. They'd come after you with pitchforks!"

He scoffs. "If I came to fetch you, they wouldn't even see me coming. You humans make so much noise but you're deaf to the world around you."

I snuggle closer to his chest and let him hold me for a while. My womb cramps painfully, and I wince, but I don't want to send Gorvor off on another mission to make me more comfortable during my courses. I'm perfectly fine here, and his affection is all the comfort I need.

"How did you get away?" he asks after a while. "Or did you end up having to marry that man?"

The tension in his big muscles tells me what he thinks of the second option, so I hurry to calm him.

"I ran away," I explain. "I stole my father's horse, rode to the first town, and sold the horse at an inn. Then I hitched a ride to a school for young ladies and begged the kitchen staff until they took me on as a scullery maid. I've been working as a maid in various establishments ever since."

Sometimes, I was lucky enough to land a job at some well-to-do house with good pay, room, and board. Other times, I made do by working at inns and guesthouses and had to pay rent for a little room of my own. Whatever it took to survive, I did it, and I could never stay in one place too long for the fear of my parents finding me. Legally, until I was married, I belonged to my father, and I don't doubt he is still searching for me. Both for the sake of me and his old horse, his most prized possessions. He'd lost both in one night, and that must have been a big blow.

I've long since lost any trace of guilt over my flight. Over *robbing* my parents of their fortune. That fortune was my life, and they would have bargained it away without a thought. It feels good to share the story with someone who is as outraged as I was about it.

"Thank you for telling me," Gorvor murmurs against my temple. "And I'm sorry you had to go through this alone."

I kiss the underside of his jaw, his stubble stinging my lips. "It brought me here in the end, didn't it?"

His arms tighten around me. "That is true."

I didn't tell him all this to garner his sympathy. There's something more I have to say, and it doesn't fall from my tongue any more easily than this confession.

"I'm sorry," I say, forcing out the words. "For treating you like I did when I first met you. I didn't know anything about orcs besides rumors, and I was horrendously rude to you and your people. Yet none of you treated me with anything but respect, better than I was ever treated by humans."

His exhale tickles my neck, and he's silent for a long moment as if he's trying to find the right words.

Then he takes my shoulders and moves me back a little to look into my eyes. "I understand now why you reacted like you did."

I snort. "You did bring some of it on yourself. I don't know that any woman would like being tossed over your shoulder like a sack of potatoes and carried into some dark tunnel."

His laugh booms through the room. "I'm an orc. I have to live up to my reputation."

"By ravaging innocent maidens, you mean?" I poke him in the chest. "You picked the wrong woman, then."

He leans his forehead against mine. "I picked exactly the right one."

Oh, he's wonderful.

I kiss him, pressing my lips against his, and we stay entwined for what seems like hours, until he is called away by his duties. After that, for the first time in my life, I allow myself to rest for no other reason than I have my courses and my belly hurts. It feels almost wrong, somehow, lazy and indulgent, but when another wave of fresh pain has me curling up in a ball, I see the wisdom in it. And the kindness that orcs apparently show their women, unlike human men, who would rather eat rusty nails than discuss a woman's courses with her.

In the afternoon, Mara shows up with my lunch and a basket full of her work correspondence. She settles down at Gorvor's writing desk, unceremoniously pushing his writing utensils to the side, and keeps me company for a while. I'm not sure whether this is her idea or Gorvor's, but when she departs in the early evening, I thank her sincerely.

"It's no bother," she says, beaming. "It hardly matters where I'm sitting when I answer the letters. Besides, you can return the favor in a week or so when *my* courses come."

On a whim, I step forward and hug her, leaning my cheek on her shoulder. With a delighted chuckle, she hugs me back, and it feels so good, having a female friend. To Mara, my pale skin doesn't matter, nor the fact that I lack tusks and the strength that distinguishes the orc race. There are so many misconceptions about orcs in the human world, and I'm ashamed that I once believed all of them.

But from now on, I can do better.

"Thank you," I whisper past a suddenly tight throat.

She draws back. "For what?"

"For being a friend," I say simply.

She clucks softly and picks up her basket. "Well, friend, see you tomorrow."

She leaves, disappearing down the dark corridor. I share the sweet rolls from my dinner with Vark and Steagor, who must be going out of their minds with boredom just standing outside my room all day. Then I close the door, settle in bed, and pull my knees to my chest.

I have a plan for making myself an indispensable part of

this clan, and I need to present it to Gorvor in a way that will make it impossible for him to deny it.

And if I'm to stay in my room and rest, this is the perfect time to think things through.

CHAPTER
THIRTEEN

"So, you see, I will need to travel to Ultrup and make connections with the local merchants. You said I could have the help of a seamstress here, but this idea won't work if I don't have a place to sell these," I say, tapping the sheet of paper on the desk.

My courses have almost ended. After four days of lying around in my bed, I'm well rested and eager to restart my duties, and especially to get this plan underway.

Gorvor looks up at me from his seat, his brow furrowed. He's been listening to me explain my business idea about the padded underwear for women, and so far, he has been nothing but supportive. My chest glows with pride and enthusiasm, because I honestly think this will be an absolute hit among human women. And with the orc clan's resources, I'll be able to produce my wares much faster than I could have if I'd set out to do this on my own.

But now the king frowns at me, his mouth a grim line. "No."

I draw back. "What do you mean, no?"

"I cannot allow you to travel to Ultrup," he says. "It is too dangerous for you."

Smoothing my hand over his black hair, I try again. "But you could send Vark and Steagor with me. They don't have other duties right now, do they? It would take me a week or two at the most, and I'd be back at your side."

Gorvor shakes his head, unyielding.

I chew on my lip, considering the issue. I hadn't counted on him rejecting my plan. Then it occurs to me. "Oh, do you want to come with me? We could travel together. Surely, Mara and the rest can hold down the fort for such a short trip."

"You are not listening to me, mate," he rumbles. "It is too dangerous for either you or me to leave the Black Bear Hill."

"But why?" I ask, my frustration rising. "Is it because of the Boar Clan orcs? Because they haven't *done* anything, not that I can see. And you can't keep me underground all the time, Gorvor. I'm not a mushroom."

The corner of his mouth twitches up. "No?"

I smack his shoulder none too gently. "You think this is a joke, but it's not. You go on your hunts all the time but leave me here under heavy guard. I feel protected, but if you insist on keeping me here, I'll start feeling like a prisoner."

"You are not a prisoner," he barks. "I am not *keeping* you here. I don't want anything to happen to you."

There's worry in his voice, and I know we're at the brink of something, a past issue so deep it's now affecting his present. *My* present. I step between his legs and bring my hands to his cheeks.

"Nothing will happen to me," I tell him. "But I'm serious. Humans need fresh air and sunshine to survive. If I remain in here all the time, I will grow sick and die."

Alarm flashes in his eyes. "What?"

I offer him a small smile. "Maybe you need a course on keeping humans, my lord?"

He gives my ass a swat. "Cheeky mate."

My smile grows into a grin. "So you'll let me go to Ultrup?"

"No. But I'll make sure you get some sunshine." Gorvor stands, picks up the paper with my plan written on it, and hands it back to me. "This is good. Just make an adjustment that will allow you to fulfill everything without having to travel."

With that, he strides out of the room, leaving me staring after him. It takes me a moment to realize he never answered my question about the strangers. And knowing Gorvor, that wasn't an accident. He's deliberately avoiding the issue, and I have no idea why.

But I intend to find out.

Over the next couple of days, I try to watch both the king and the Boar Clan orcs. Their movements are nothing out of the ordinary, apart from the fact that everyone seems to be avoiding the strangers, going out of their way to not have to interact with them. If they're so unwanted, why does Gorvor allow them to remain here? Our warriors are strong, and the strangers are outnumbered severely, since there are only four of them.

Something is wrong, and tensions are rising with each passing day, each meal eaten in the presence of the four smirking orcs who seem to delight in being a disruptive presence in our great hall. I dislike them on principle, even though I've never spoken to them, because they leer at the women and follow them with greedy, insolent gazes. I notice that the orc males from the Black Bear Clan are becoming increasingly protective of women of all ages, and I feel like it's only a matter of time before this blows up.

I don't want that to happen, not when it's most likely to be a vicious fight smack in the middle of a crowded communal space, filled with families, children, and the elderly. I try to pry information from Mara, as well as from Vark and Steagor, but they're all tight-lipped about it and don't hesitate to show their frustration with my continued questioning.

Gorvor listens to me, however, and organizes a picnic for the two of us in a sunny clearing not far from the Black Bear Hill's main gate. We walk there under the green canopies of the spring-lush trees and sit in a meadow studded with fragrant wildflowers. At the same time, a full contingent of guards take their posts in a wide perimeter, their watchful dark eyes darting this way and that, searching for some unseen threat. One of the males, Bogur, is even sent to scout farther afield to make sure nothing can surprise us.

It's a nice gesture, and I enjoy my time in the sun, lying on my back on the blanket until I'm hot and sweaty in my dress, but it's not the relaxing, intimate outing I'd envisioned for the two of us. Maybe I'm delusional, thinking the king can leave whenever he wishes, without guards, with just his mate by his side, and yet that's what I wanted. Then we return to the Hill, to the darkness of its corridors, and the bright, warm sunshine is replaced by the feeble glow of my lantern.

I don't want to complain to Mara during my visit to her room when her courses come, so I throw myself into work, helping her by answering letters, ordering supplies, and communicating with the kitchen staff to settle on the menus for the following weeks. She records everything in a large, leather-bound ledger, her pen strokes assured and neat.

"I'll be right back," she says, stretching. "I think I'm ready for a quick bath, and then we can work on those farming reports."

She places the ledger on the bed and walks to the bathroom niche, closing the tapestry behind her. I finish scribbling out a list of supplies we'll need for a hunting trip that Gorvor and his men are planning for next week—they'll be hunting wild sheep higher up in the mountains and will be gone for three days at least. I try not to chafe at the fact that the king is allowed to leave the Hill while I must remain here, but I don't want to bring Mara into the argument, so I haven't said anything to her yet.

Still, I need to know how much money we'll need to put aside for the provisions, so I reach for the ledger. If I search through Mara's detailed notes, I can figure out the cost of items on my own without even having to ask.

I place the heavy book in my lap and leaf a couple of pages back, searching for the right entries. This is a running list of all the clan's expenses and income, a record of all the trading we do with both humans and orcs from other clans. Most are for small sums, six gold marks for thirty-five wolverine pelts sold, a handful of coppers for a hundred pounds of rye. I note down the prices for aged cheese and apples, wondering if there's a stream nearby where we could catch any fish, because buying and salting our own is costing us a fortune...

I skim over a line with my finger and pause.

The sum is what stalls me, five hundred gold marks paid. It's larger than any other note in the ledger by a factor of ten, and the subject of the trade is only marked by five vertical lines.

What...?

Then it hits me. Five lines. Five hundred marks.

Five people.

I scan the date quickly, wondering if it corresponds to the date when I arrived at the Black Bear Hill. It doesn't. It's an earlier entry, and paging through the ledger, I find another line from around the time I was bought at auction. Three hundred and eighty marks, with four lines marking our souls.

I wonder how much they paid for me, for a young, relatively attractive woman of good health, and how much for the boy they eventually returned to his family. How much was I worth? And have I earned out their investment yet?

Nothing you've done here so far is worth that much money.

They're ugly thoughts I shouldn't be thinking. I knew my release from the slave pens in Ultrup was the result of a simple transaction, but it hurts so much to see it on paper, a cold number attached to living, thinking beings.

I glance over my shoulder to where the bathroom tapestry is still closed, hiding Mara from view. I turn the pages faster now, searching for more purchases of human slaves. In my time here, I've only met the gloomy human healer in the infirmary, and the warriors who brought me here haven't departed on any new trips to town yet. Still, I wonder where all these humans have ended up—because I count seventeen more inky strikes, representing seventeen people, noted in the past two and a half years.

But as I leaf through pages and pages of Mara's diligent notes, a niggling thought enters my mind. The sums paid for humans all revolve in the hundreds, which is a lot of money. With so many people bought, the tally I do in my head quickly brings me to several thousand gold marks.

And yet, the money coming in from the trade of fur,

mead, weapons, and other small items that orcs provide for the humans is not nearly enough to pay for such exorbitant purchases.

The numbers don't add up.

"Oh!"

An exclamation from behind me has me jumping in place, and I curl my fingers protectively around the ledger's leather cover. Then I turn and face Mara, who stands in the middle of her room, her usually bright-green face now ashen.

"You shouldn't be looking through that," she says, and her voice trembles a little.

She extends her hand, motioning for me to hand over the book, but I tuck it against my chest.

"Why not?" I challenge. "Is it because you're worried I might see how much you paid for me?"

Her face crumples, and she sinks heavily on the bed beside me. "I'm sorry," she croaks. "I didn't want you to know. It's... It's so ugly."

Her brown eyes are shiny with unshed tears, and she gazes at me imploringly. But that shell around my heart is hardening again, working to protect me.

"I guess I should be grateful," I say, the words hollow. "That someone thought I was worth all that money."

She grabs my arm, her fingers digging into my muscles. "That number has *nothing* to do with your worth, Dawn. Nothing."

I shrug her off, unable to bear her touch, and jump to my feet. "Yes, but if the price for me was set higher, at two hundred marks. Maybe three hundred? Would the warriors who came to town still have purchased me?" I pace, the heels of my boots scuffing on the hard-packed earth. "Or would it be a matter of cold, simple math to determine who they can buy for the least amount of money? How many slaves are left in those barracks every time? I got out because I'm young and able-bodied, but there were people in there who are going to horrible places."

Tears run down my face, but I don't care, because this hurts so much. It's all the old hurt from my parents' decision to sell me for profit, combined with the horrors I've seen—and avoided by some strange stroke of luck—at the auction house.

"Let me call Gorvor," Mara pleads. "He'll tell you it's not like that. He's been working so hard to make any progress with the slavery laws."

I let out a harsh laugh, but it turns into a sob halfway. "Gorvor won't tell me anything. He never does."

She falls silent, biting her lip, and some inner part of me twinges with guilt. She's not to blame for this, for any of this. Mara is not responsible for the abhorrent slave trade that plagues the land of Styria, nor is she the one who buys humans at auction in town. No, she just records the numbers in her ledger, detached from it all.

I turn on her and wave the ledger in her direction. "Why don't the numbers add up?" I demand.

She blinks. "What?"

I tap the cover impatiently. "The numbers. They don't add up. Where is the money for the slaves coming from?"

If possible, she pales even more—or turns gray, which passes for the same thing with orcs. "I don't know."

She's lying. I haven't known her for long, but Mara hasn't lied to me up until now. She has refused to tell me things, yes, and she is adept at changing the subject whenever I get too close to something she's not supposed to discuss with me, but this denial is a flat-out lie.

I take another step toward her. I'm shorter than her by

several inches, but with her sitting on the bed, I glower down at her. "Mara, where is the money coming from?"

She presses her lips together and hangs her head.

"Fine." I throw the ledger on her bed, where it bounces and comes to rest on top of some crumpled correspondence. "I'll find out somehow."

With that, I twist around and stride for the door.

"Dawn," she calls, her voice pleading.

But I don't listen. I stomp into the corridor, where Vark and Steagor come to attention on either side of me. I look from one to the other. "Take me to your king."

FOURTEEN

Vark tries to strike up a conversation while we march through the dark corridors, but I remain silent, fuming over what I've discovered. We pass several orcs, including the scout I met the other day, and they call out greetings, but for once, I don't bother returning them. Gorvor said they were saving humans from the slave trade, offering them positions in the orc settlements if they had nowhere else to go. But how did they finance these rescue missions? And why was everyone being so secretive about it?

My footsteps echo through the halls, but Vark's and Steagor's are nearly silent. They're like wolves on the prowl, watching my every move and alert to any danger that might pop up. This alone should have been enough for me to question our situation. If I'm safe inside the Hill and Gorvor doesn't want me to travel to the human towns, it's very strange that I need armed escort in here.

Nothing adds up, and I've had it with the non-answers and half-truths. With the outright lies.

Steagor stops in front of a heavily reinforced wooden door and bangs his fist on it.

"Where are we?" I ask.

"The armory," Vark answers. "The king is inspecting the newest batch of weapons from our forge. Neekar and Ozork are leaving for town soon and will be taking a load with them."

My stomach twists at this information. Will the orcs return with more displaced, purchased humans?

I don't have the time to think the question through because the door swings open, and Ozork appears at the threshold.

"The queen would speak to the king," Steagor announces in his gruff, deep voice.

Ozork ducks back into the room, and a moment later, reappears with Neekar in tow. The younger orc exclaims at the sight of me, stomps closer, and wraps me in a tight hug. His strong arms crush me to his chest, and he laughs loudly.

"Hello, Dawn," he exclaims. "I see you have adjusted well. The king looks happy. I was sorry you weren't meant to be my mate, but the gods know best, eh? You are so beautiful, my queen."

He releases me from his stranglehold and holds me out in front of him. Heat rises in my cheeks at his blatant but entirely friendly appreciation.

Then I remember he's a part of this nasty business, and I sober up, withdrawing from him.

"Get your hands away from my mate, soldier," the king growls from behind Neekar.

My warrior friend half turns to look back at Gorvor, and I peer around him to find the king standing in the doorway, his arms crossed over his massive chest. Even though I'm so much smaller than him, I forget how big he is sometimes— even compared to other orcs. He's wearing his crown today, the cold iron glinting in the light of my lantern and the torches lit inside the room.

From his words, I expected him to glower at Neekar, but apparently, he knows that his subordinate is harmless to me, because he wears a reluctant grin on his handsome face. My stomach twists at the sight.

I've fallen in love with him, and I didn't even notice. The feelings crept up on me, worming their way into my heart without my permission. And I've been enjoying it so much, glowing under his attention and care. Now I have to face the possibility that he's doing something nefarious and wrong to obtain the human slaves. Maybe he sells them on. Maybe he robs innocent people of their livelihood to finance his operation. I have no idea what's going on, only that nothing makes sense.

"If she was my mate, I'd never let her out of my sight," Neekar taunts the king, smiling wickedly. "And she also wouldn't want me to leave. She would want me at her side always."

Ozork grabs Neekar by his neck and pushes him down the corridor, past me and my guards. "You have spent too much time in the company of women who are paid to tell you sweet lies, my friend."

Vark snickers, and Neekar protests loudly, but his words are lost because Ozork drags him around the corner. I watch them leave, stalling. I've come here to have a painful conversation with my mate, and yet now, I don't want to start.

Maybe I don't want to know what he has to tell me. Maybe the truth will prove too painful, and I'm better off not knowing.

Then I square my shoulders and turn on my heels, facing him. I need to find out what's going on. I owe it to all the people the orcs have bought at auction—and everyone they've left. I owe it to *myself*.

Gorvor extends his hand to me. "Hello, little mate. Did you miss me? Is that why you've come?"

I walk to him and place my hand in his. His palm swallows mine as he draws me into the large room. The guards remain stationed outside, but the king closes the door and slides the bolts across, giving us privacy.

He backs me up against the iron-reinforced oakwood and dips his face to my neck, inhaling sharply. My gaze falls past him to the walls, teeming with axes and longbows, to the racks of swords and spears, to the shields stacked high. Enough steel to outfit an army.

"I've been thinking about you all day. About the way you rode me this morning. My cock has been harder than forged steel, and I've had to pretend I was interested in axes." He presses a kiss to my neck. "And daggers." Another kiss. "And swords."

I lean my head back on the door, giving him better access. I can't help it—the effect he has on me is potent and instantaneous.

"Ah, I smell your pussy getting wet." He groans, rocking his hips against my belly. "I need to have you."

His cock is as hard as he says, a ridge straining behind the laces of his leather pants, and it would be so easy to let myself forget all about my questions and fall into passion with him. He drives me wild. Our bodies are made for each other, made to bring out the highest, most exquisite pleasure.

He reaches for the hem of my skirts, flipping them up with ease that speaks of practice, because we've done this a lot over the past weeks. I grasp his shoulders to push him away, but my traitorous fingers dig in, pulling him in for a kiss. Gorvor devours my mouth, his hot tongue stroking mine, and in a dizzying move, he picks me up with one arm and deposits me on a work bench, scattering whetstones and bits of leather to the floor.

He wedges himself between my legs, his thick thighs spreading me rudely. With his free hand, he reaches up and swipes his fingers through my pussy without warning.

I cry out, the sensations threatening to pitch me into a swift, intense climax.

But they're also enough to snap me out of this haze of lust. I release Gorvor's shoulders, jerk back, and shove at his chest.

"Wait," I gasp.

He stills, his hand cupping me. "What is it?"

I screw my eyes shut, attempting to dispel the effect he has on me. "We need to talk."

He kisses me again, a brutal claiming. "We can talk after."

"No, Gorvor." I break the kiss and force myself to look him in the eyes. "I saw Mara's ledger."

His shoulders bunch with tension, but he still doesn't release me. He's clothed, and yet my skirts are rucked up, my naked thighs spread.

"I need to know where the money for the slaves is coming from." My voice is quiet, but it doesn't tremble, and I'm grateful. I sound more self-assured than I am. "The accounts don't add up. Your clan—*our* clan—isn't making enough money to buy all those people through normal trade."

He frowns down at me, his grip tightening on my waist. "So?"

"So? What is it that you're hiding?" I exclaim, frustration rising in my chest. On the short walk to the armory, I'd gone through so many possibilities, discarding one after another, and only one thing makes sense. "Are you trading those people on to earn a profit? Are you using them for slave labor to finance the purchases? Tell me!"

His gaze darkens, and he crowds closer to me. "You think I'm no better than a slave trader?"

"No! I mean, I don't know." I push his hands away and cover myself with my skirts. My throat closes up, but I need to get this out. "It's just that no one tells me anything, so I'm left to draw my own conclusions. And they're not good."

"What we do is none of your concern," he growls. "You haven't been here long enough to know how it was before. What we've had to do to protect our people."

My eyes prickle with tears, and I hate that, I hate it so much. I've lost myself here, lost the will to escape, to free myself, because someone—this orc—showed me kindness. For the first time in my life, someone treated me well, and I mistook that for deeper feelings. For respect.

How wrong I was.

"Your reasoning is flawed." I sniffle and dash the hem of my sleeve over my eyes. "Everything that happens here is my concern. If I participated in keeping humans enslaved, I couldn't live with myself. Even if I did it unknowingly."

The king growls, turning away from me. His shoulders rise and fall with angry, quick breaths. "So you have decided we are guilty? Even though I told you we were saving humans?"

I throw my hands up. "But that's all you ever do! You *tell* me how things are. It's your word against the numbers in your ledger, my lord. You never gave me a shred of proof that the humans you bought and paid for were happy to remain here and work for you."

He twists in his pacing, and suddenly he's in front of me, cupping the back of my head. "Are you not the proof? Have you been mistreated? Are you not happy?"

I bite my lip because I can't deny it. The first time I've known happiness in my adult life was here, in the Black Bear Hill, with Gorvor—and with Mara, the guards, and the other orcs who have gone out of their way to make me feel welcome.

And yet...

"I'm not free," I whisper. "You bought me, you had me brought to you, and yes, I've been safe and fed and cherished. But I am not free, Gorvor."

He scowls. "Of course you are. You have the run of the settlement. You chose your own work. I have *never* forced you into anything."

"But you won't let me leave!" I shove my finger into his massive chest. "I asked you to let me travel to town, and you forbade it. When I said I needed sunlight to survive, you arranged it, but the guards followed us closely, and you picked the route, the spot where we stopped, and the duration of our outing."

He catches my hand and grips it, hard. "I did that to *protect* you. If you knew what could happen to you—"

"What?" I lean in, imploring him with my eyes. "Tell me. Are you afraid I'd get gored by a wild boar? That I'd fall into a ditch and break my neck? Believe it or not, I survived just fine without you for twenty-six years."

"And then you got snatched by slavers," he roars. He closes his eyes, takes a deep breath, and adds in a calmer voice, "My men told me about the state you were in when they bought you."

I rear back, stung. "A-are you saying it's *my* fault I was kidnapped?"

"No!" He pushes his fingers into his hair, frustration radiating from him. "Only that you need someone to take care of you."

I press my lips together, too angry to worry about crying anymore. "Well, then. Good thing you came along to tell me how I should live my life."

Twisting away from him, I march to the door and put all my strength into throwing open the heavy bolts. It's a strain, and it infuriates me even more, because it's making me look incompetent and weak. But I don't give up, and the iron slides to the side with a snick.

"Dawn," Gorvor says, his voice quiet. "Don't."

But I've had enough of listening to him for one day. I open the door wide—and find myself staring at Vark and Steagor, who shuffle away quickly with guilty expressions on their faces.

They must have been eavesdropping this entire time. Not that they would have had to strain their ears, with orc hearing being as good as it is.

I lift my head high, though shame burns through me, and start down the corridor in the direction from where we came. Only a short time has passed, yet everything feels different. None of my questions were answered, and I have broken, perhaps irreparably, my relationship with the king.

It takes me only a minute to realize I've left my lantern at the armory. The glow of the torches fades behind us, and I find myself standing in pitch-black darkness, surrounded on all sides by damp earth of the tunnel. Suddenly, my breath comes short, my heart thundering. I'm lost, completely.

A warm hand closes around mine, and Vark's voice comes from the darkness to my left. "Here, my lady. Hold on to me."

I grasp his elbow and let him lead me through the corridors. Behind us, Steagor follows, his footsteps soft. And I let my tears fall, because I can't hold them back anymore. My orc guards, my constant shadows, must see them, but neither one of them says a thing.

We arrive at the king's chamber, and Steagor opens the door for me. Light spills from the room, and the single lantern I left burning that morning now seems bright as the sun.

For the first time, Steagor bows to me, his brown eyes full of understanding. "Our king is good," he rumbles in his deep voice, as if he's unused to voicing such opinions. "The life we had before was...hard. We owe him a lot."

I stare up at him, trying to understand. "But what happened before? Why won't anyone talk about it?"

Steagor shakes his head. "It's not my story to tell."

Bitterness rises inside me. "Yes, yes, everyone keeps saying that. But the person whose story it is won't talk to me."

Defeated, I bid my guards goodnight and shut myself in the room. And when Gorvor comes in much later, I pretend to be asleep when he brushes my hair from my face, so gentle I could cry. It takes everything in me to keep myself from screwing up my face and to remain relaxed and unresponsive.

And when he wraps his warm, heavy arm around me and tucks me close to his chest, my heart cracks even more.

Only when his breathing deepens, hot against the back of my neck, do I allow myself to cry, the tears soaking my pillow.

CHAPTER
FIFTEEN

Gorvor is gone by the time I wake the next morning, and his side of the bed is long cold. I try not to let it get to me, but it's impossible. My head feels too heavy, my thoughts sluggish and dark. I bathe, washing my tears away with the warm water, and feel marginally better afterward.

Still, it's a long, painful day. I cannot work with Mara after yesterday's incident, so I make myself useful in the kitchen, even roping Vark into helping me chop a mound of root vegetables for tonight's stew. We send Steagor off to rest, because we're surrounded by so many friendly orcs, and I feel bad for taking over my guards' life completely— even though I wasn't the one who assigned them to this duty.

I putter around the kitchen, washing massive cauldrons and kneading dough, glazing honey cakes and sweeping the floor, until I'm swaying with fatigue. Vark keeps up with me and at the end of the after-dinner cleanup, picks me up bodily and carries me back to the king's chamber. I collapse on the bed, still dressed, and sink into a deep sleep, and the next morning, I repeat it all, disheartened by the empty bed beside me.

I catch glimpses of Gorvor through the kitchen door at mealtimes, speaking with his scouts or other warriors, but I don't join him at the big table. I prefer to take my meals by the counter in the kitchen, tearing chunks of still-warm bread with my teeth while trying to hide from prying eyes. I think by now, everyone in Black Bear Hill has caught on to the fact that the king and I are arguing, so they're tiptoeing around me, casting me worried glances.

And I don't resent them for it—in fact, the last thing I want is to discuss my relationship with anyone. Because Gorvor and I aren't *arguing*. We're just ignoring each other to see who will crack first.

I'm sure the king expects me to fold and submit to his ridiculous rules. He wants to keep me in this anthill of a town, barefoot and pregnant, as the saying goes.

And I might be. Pregnant, that is. I'd forgotten all about the tea mixes Gorvor got for me that first week, and the timing might be right. We haven't had sex in days, but if I counted the days right, my life could get a lot more complicated soon.

Still, I won't break. I have survived on my own for more than a decade, and I won't shy away from hard work. In fact, on the third morning, I seek out Mara, who looks like she hasn't had much sleep lately, and ask what the wages are for a kitchen maid. The sum she gives me is fair, if small, and I calculate it will take me *years* to pay off the hundred gold marks that the orcs paid for me at the auction. Still, if I work two shifts a day, I can halve the time easily and be out of here soon after.

Mara's eyes water when I ask her to keep a tally of my earnings.

"You don't have to pay anything back," she whispers. "That's not how it works."

I stare at her. "Then how *does* it work? You do all this out of the goodness of your hearts?"

She presses her hand to her mouth and shakes her head but doesn't say anything.

"Right," I say. "Not your place. Just keep that running total for me, please."

I depart from her office, even more heartbroken than before.

Still, the tensions rise in the Hill, with more warriors coming and going, meetings held in secret that either Vark or Steagor must attend, and a scuffle erupts between one of the Boar Clan males and a young orc whose sister was the object of some rude remark. I marvel at the fact that the strangers are allowed to remain here despite everything, but now I keep my thoughts to myself and continue watching and listening for any hint of what's going on.

I return to our bedchamber one evening, tired to the bone, to find Gorvor sitting on the bed with a small wooden chest beside him. I stop, unsure of what to do. We've been avoiding each other, and he has taken to coming to bed late and rising early, so we haven't spoken in a week.

But now he's here, shirtless and beautiful, his broad shoulders hunched in a way I haven't seen before. I stop on the threshold, hesitating. Then something nudges me from behind. I glance over my shoulder to find Steagor shooing me forward. I raise my eyebrows at him, and he nods, encouraging, then gives me another, harder push that sends me stumbling forward. Before I can do anything, he grabs the side of the door and pulls it shut, cutting me away from my only escape route.

It's nothing new, being kept somewhere I don't want to

be, but I'm shocked Steagor cares enough to meddle in our affairs. I glower at the door for a moment, deciding whether it's worth opening it and giving the hulking orc a piece of my mind. But if Gorvor is here, maybe he wants to talk...

I twist around and stop. He's looking at me, his black eyes solemn. For once, he doesn't move a muscle, just waits, his large hands gripping the covers by his sides.

Finally, I can't take the silence anymore. "I'm tired," I say. "I'm going to get ready for bed."

He gives me a slow nod, then turns to the side and picks up the wooden box. "Here."

He holds it out to me, waiting.

Curious in spite of myself, I walk closer and wrap my fingers around the handles at the sides. Gorvor lets go, and I nearly drop the box, that's how heavy it is. Struggling with its weight, I carry it over to the writing desk. Its insides rattle when I drop it heavily onto the cluttered surface.

"What is this?" I ask.

Gorvor motions for me to open it.

I unclasp the simple mechanism at the front and open the lid. My breath rushes from me on a surprised exhale.

It's money.

And a lot of it. Yellow gold marks, each coin heavy and large, are crammed inside, filling the small chest's entire space. I've never seen so much gold in my life.

I glance up at Gorvor, who has come to stand beside me. I have so many questions, my mind can't seem to decide on just one, so I gape at him in silence.

"It's a hundred and fifty marks," he says, his voice low. "Consider it...your dowry."

I swallow, my throat dry. "I think the bride's family is supposed to provide a dowry, not the groom's."

He makes an impatient gesture with his hand. "Then it's a wedding gift. I don't care what you call it."

I close the lid, hiding the shiny coins from view. "Why would you give this to me? I have nowhere to spend it. And why now?"

A muscle ticks in his jaw, and in the dim light of the single lantern illuminating the room, he seems...tired. Like he hasn't slept enough in a while. Like maybe he has been working too much and spreading himself too thin.

"Mara told me about your agreement," he says slowly. "That she would keep a tally of your wages for you."

I straighten my shoulders. "Oh, is that it? You don't want me to be paid?"

He shakes his head. "No, Dawn. I wanted you to know that you didn't owe me anything. Or the clan. So I'm giving you a wedding gift. I should have gotten you something before, but...orcs don't put much stock in things like that."

No, they don't. I've learned through my time here that vanity is not an orc trait, and that jewelry and adornments are seen as fussy and impractical, more than anything.

"Like I told you," Gorvor continues, "it's a hundred and fifty gold marks."

Something clicks inside my brain. "Is that... Is that how much...?"

I can't force the words out. A lump forms in my throat, and I clench my jaw, forcing myself to keep calm.

"Aye. That was how much Neekar and Ozork paid for you at the auction." Gorvor takes my shoulders gently and turns me so we're facing each other. "That is *not* how much you are worth. I would pay a hundred times that for your freedom. A thousand. If only you would find your way to me again."

I can't stop the tears from slipping down my cheeks. He

brushes them away with his big thumbs, then takes hold of my chin and lifts it so I'm forced to look him in the eyes.

"Pick up the chest and give it to me, Dawn," he orders.

I swipe my sleeve over my face and take hold of the heavy load. "Why?"

He motions with his hand. "Give it to me."

I extend my shaking arms and offer him the chest. He accepts it and drops it back on the desk with a heavy thud. "Now you have paid what you thought was your debt. You owe me *nothing*, do you understand?"

I manage to nod, but my face crumples, so I cover it with my hands, sobbing. Strong arms wrap around me, and Gorvor squeezes me to his warm chest, muttering soothing nonsense in my ear. He caresses my hair and eventually, when he realizes I'm not calming down anytime soon, he carries me over to the bed and tucks me under the covers, douses the lantern, and gets in behind me.

I fight sleep, not wanting to give up the sensation of being in his arms again. I don't know if this strange conversation will fix anything between us, yet I don't want to let go.

But exhaustion pulls me under, the cost of working as much as I did over the past week finally catching up with me.

"Stay," I mumble, fighting through the fog of dreams.

Gorvor's arms tighten around me. "I'll stay, little mate. Now sleep."

SIXTEEN

I wake feeling warm and well rested, and it takes me a moment to realize that the source of warmth is my mate, curled protectively around me. I can't tell yet if he's awake or not, so I lie motionless, not wanting to disturb him. He likely needed this rest as much as I did, judging by his appearance last night.

"Good morning," he rumbles, his breath fanning the fine hairs on my neck.

I bite my lip, then roll in place to face him. "Hello."

He brings his forehead to mine and closes his eyes. "I missed this."

My heart squeezes painfully, and I bring my palm to his stubbled cheek. "Me, too."

He didn't set everything right last night by clearing what I'd thought was my debt, but he tried to help me in his own way. And I can't stay angry with him. I love him, and that might make me stupid and vulnerable, but I don't want our lives to continue like we've been living them for the past week.

Gorvor turns his face into my touch and kisses my palm.

I suppress a shiver that runs through my body, but he must feel it regardless, because he fixes me with a hot stare. I widen my eyes, caught in his attention like a startled hare.

If he kisses me right now, I'll kiss him back. I've missed him so much—not only his body but the time we spent together, the two of us, enjoying our bond.

But Gorvor shakes himself, utters a foul curse under his breath, and throws off the covers, hopping to his feet. His speed and agility still surprise me, because he shouldn't be this quick with that massive body of his. I should have learned by now not to judge orcs by human standards, though.

"Come," he says. "We must wash, and then I want to show you something."

He tugs me toward the bathing pool, turns me away from him, and helps me out of my wrinkled dress with efficient tugs. I strip naked, no longer self-conscious around him, and slip into the water, scrubbing myself quickly.

Gorvor stands at the edge of the pool for a long moment, glowering at me, then shoves down his leather pants and kicks them into a corner. My mouth waters at the sight of him, erect and thick, but he seems to be ignoring his...situation, so I do my best to imitate him. Still, I can't help but remember how good he feels when he sinks inside me, and I squeeze my legs together to keep my arousal in check.

Gorvor's nostrils flare, and he sends me a frustrated look. "Stop that. We have somewhere to be."

In spite of everything that happened between us, I can't stifle a giggle. He's clearly lusting after me as much as I am for him, and I don't need inhumanly good senses to see it. He groans as he washes himself. I can only imagine how it must feel to drag his palm over his hard cock but not finish the job.

But when he motions at me to climb out of the pool, I obey him, drying myself quickly. He does the same, then helps me with a fresh dress, doing up my laces.

"Where are we going?" I ask as he throws open the door.

"You'll see."

Gorvor faces Vark and Steagor, stationed by the door. They're talking to that scout, Bogur, and he sketches a little bow toward the king, then leaves, as if he wants to give us privacy.

"You can take the morning off," Gorvor tells the guards. "I will be escorting Dawn."

Vark straightens his shoulders. "Do you think that's wise? The Boar Clan—"

"Won't follow us where we're going," the king interrupts. "Please."

The guards exchange a glance, then disappear into the darkness of the corridor. I lift my eyebrows at Gorvor, but he shakes his head, still not telling me anything.

"Take your lantern," he instructs. "You'll need it where we're going."

More intrigued than ever, I check the oil in the lantern, light the wick, and follow him through the maze of tunnels. After a long, meandering corridor with many closed doors and branching pathways, we leave behind the earthen tunnels and enter a part of the Hill I've never been to before. It's hewn from rock and must have been the work of many generations working tirelessly to create it.

I glance at Gorvor's back in front of me, wondering if it was his ancestors who dug out this place. He has never mentioned his family, and I haven't pried—but now that feels like a mistake on my part. He's my mate, yet I don't know anything beyond his father's name, and that only because Gorvor had introduced himself to me as 'son of Trak.'

Finally, we reach a steep staircase and climb in a dizzying spiral. My lantern is the only thing that lights the way, and after a while, I get the impression we're stuck on an endless staircase and the world around us has disappeared, leaving us stranded here forever.

But at last, the light falls on a landing, and after another short flight of stairs, we end up in a narrow corridor with a single wooden door at the end. It's lower than the other doorways in the Hill, more human-sized than most. Gorvor produces a black iron key from his weapons belt and unlocks the bolt. Then he stands aside and motions for me to enter.

I push the door open and step over the threshold. The room beyond isn't large, but it's well furnished and cozy, with fur rugs lining the stone floor and a small fireplace that now stands cold but would light up the place and warm it. A trickle of water has me looking to my left, and I follow it to find a bathing area with water running from a stone spout into a trough-like sink. But when I put my hand under the stream, expecting the warmth of the thermal water, I shiver—it's icy-cold and clear.

Leaning in, I cup the water in my hands and take a sip. It's clean, almost sweet-tasting, and reminds me of the water the kitchen staff have funneled through pipes to fill pots and scrub the heavy pans.

"This is where my mother used to live," Gorvor says quietly.

I straighten and face him. He stands in the middle of the room, his hands on his hips, and surveys the space with an almost melancholic gaze. Then he strides to a wall tapestry depicting a hunting scene, jerks it aside, and reveals window shutters, twin oakwood panes closing in a large window. After some fumbling and a big *creak*, Gorvor throws them open, and golden sunlight floods inside.

I gasp, moving forward before I realize what I'm doing. "Oh! This is…"

My words stall in my throat as I take in the scene before me. Through the tunnels inside the Hill, we must have ascended some sort of cliff, because below us, a wall of sheer rock falls toward the forest canopy, which is stretched out like a dark-green carpet. I crane my neck to look up and find more gray rock, so steep it would be impossible to climb.

"When we moved into the Hill, it took us a long time to discover all the hidden nooks," Gorvor says. "We don't know who delved as high or as deep as these places go. Orcs usually live underground, but this was beyond anything we'd ever seen. The whole settlement was abandoned, and we worked hard to make it habitable over the years."

Pride shines through his words. I can imagine them arriving in this place for the first time, finding the great hall, the chambers, the thermal springs. I take his hand and squeeze his fingers, acknowledging his words but allowing him to continue.

"My mother was…unhappy that she was stuck underground." His smile is rueful and more than a little sad now. "She was human, like you."

"What? But you're so…" I motion with my hand to encompass everything about him. "You're such an *orc*."

He huffs out a laugh. "That's how it works with orcs and humans. We don't have as many children as humans do, but whenever we mate with them, our offspring take after us."

He pauses and gives me a meaningful look. And I get it. If we had children, I would bear him orc sons or daughters. A few weeks ago, that thought would have terrified me. But now... I've seen happy orc families with pudgy, green-skinned orc babies, and I want one of my own.

I smile up at Gorvor and give his hand another squeeze. "All right, so your mother was human."

He leads me over to the bed and motions for me to sit, then sinks onto the edge beside me. "Aye. But my father was an orc." He makes an impatient sound in his throat. "Obviously. I'm making a mess out of this."

I put my hand on his leather-clad knee. "It's fine. Just take it slowly."

I'm not sure why he brought me here, but he's opening up to me, so I won't do anything to discourage him.

He covers my hand with his and lets out a deep sigh. "My father is the king of the Boar Clan."

His words are laced with so much venom, I flinch involuntarily. "Really?"

"My mother was his—" He stops himself and lowers his head, a muscle twitching in his jaw.

And suddenly, everything becomes clear. The wild, expensive purchases at the auction house. His reaction when I accused him of selling the humans for profit.

"She was his slave?" I venture softly.

He dips his head in a nod. "She was only twenty-two when he bought her. That they were mates is clear because I was the product of their bond, but he was never good to her. Never gentle. She was..."

He trails off again, and his throat bobs as he swallows. My

stomach threatens to revolt, because I can only imagine what a rude, violent orc can do to a young woman. When Gorvor and I first joined together in bed, it was a long night before we both found pleasure. What would have happened if Gorvor hadn't been so gentle and patient with me? And I with him?

"You don't have to tell me," I say. "I'm here if you do, but I understand enough. There's no need to put it into words if you don't want to."

He sends me a grateful look, and his grip on me tightens. "She never spoke about it with me. And she did try to shield me from the worst of his violence."

He rubs his hand over his scarred chest, and now I see the many silvery scars in a new light. Gorvor grew up to be a great warrior, but as a child, he'd been vulnerable.

"I'm so sorry," I whisper. "That must have been horrible."

He lifts one shoulder in a gesture that should portray indifference, but he doesn't quite get away with it. "She stopped speaking to me when I was about twelve. I think I reminded her too much of my father."

I press my lips together because I don't want to cry. I feel for the young orc who must have been so confused by his mother's refusal, and yet I cannot find it in me to hate the poor woman who'd had no choice in her life.

Gorvor clears his throat, his gaze on his lap. "Charan of Boar Clan, the male you heard speak at our mating celebration. He is my younger brother."

"By the same mother?" I blurt out, then cover my mouth with my hand. "Of course he is. Only mates can produce offspring."

Gorvor nods. "My father's kingdom is large. He is a powerful ruler and he leads many orcs. He has waged wars with other orc kingdoms and taken over their lands, one by one. I was his heir."

He absentmindedly rubs his thumb over my wrist, and I feel every callous on his work-roughened palm.

"A little over a decade ago, I gathered around me a following of orcs who didn't want to go on serving him," he continues. "The wars took a toll on the clan. We were strong and wealthy, but at what cost? So many males lost at the front. So many children left fatherless. But the king wouldn't stop."

I notice that he calls him *the king*, not his father. I don't think he's aware of the distinction, but it's an important one.

"So you left?" I ask.

"That would have been too easy." He scoffs. "I fought him. To the death, he'd said. But after I bested him, my mother asked me to let him live. He was her mate. She hated him, but she couldn't let him die."

Gorvor scrubs a hand over his face, and I can almost taste his pain. Maybe it's the bond growing stronger between us or plain sympathy, but my heart hurts for him just the same. I try to imagine a younger version of him, standing up to his tormentor.

"I let him live," he goes on. "And I thought he would be grateful I didn't kill him and take over the Boar Clan. That's what he would have done. He saw my mercy as weakness. But we wanted nothing to do with the lands he'd bought with the blood of our people. The kingdom had grown *too* large and unwieldy to manage. So we offered everyone who wanted to leave a fresh start. And we left."

"Your mother," I say. "She went with you, then?"

Gorvor grimaces. "She did. But she wasn't herself. And

she didn't live long after she separated herself from my father."

That must have been horrible to watch, his mother wasting away because she left her own abuser.

"And you found this place by chance?" I don't want to dig into his pain, but I still have questions about his life.

He shakes his head. "No, Ozork found it when he'd been scouting past the human lands. The Boar Clan's territory and ours is separated by a strip of human-controlled ground. The city of Ultrup is a part of it, and humans would marshal all their forces if an orc army ever stepped foot over the border. That's what's been keeping my father from following us and killing us all."

It's a chilling statement. Knowing that only the relative might of the human empire stands between us and a marauding orc army does nothing to calm my nerves.

"So why do you allow Charan and his warriors to stay here?" I demand. "They have been causing trouble for everyone."

A muscle ticks in Gorvor's jaw. "He is my brother. He arrived here mere days before you and claimed our father was ailing. I remain heir apparent. If he dies, his kingdom would fall under my rule. Charan wants it for himself, of course. He remained behind when I left and took the brunt of our father's anger and violence in my stead."

I wince, imagining what that must have been like. "But you still don't want that kingdom?"

"No. We have everything we need here. Our trade routes are established and our relationship with the current lord of Ultrup is improving." He gives me a small smile and nudges me gently with his elbow. "We're a long way from outlawing slavery, but we do what we can."

I remember the day I first met Mara. She'd told me

about the king's attempts to stop the abominable practice of snatching humans who had no one to protect them. Humans like me. Tears gather in my eyes, and I lean my forehead against his chest. "I'm sorry I thought you were trading people."

He brings his arm around my shoulders and tucks me into his side. "You had no way of knowing. Your reasoning was sound, Dawn."

"Still, I almost caused an irreparable rift between us." I peer up at him. "I could have ruined this."

He frowns. "I never would have given up on you. You are my mate."

I go on my knees beside him. "And you are mine."

His dark eyes heat with passion, and we tear at each other's clothes in a race to see how fast he can get inside me. He pulls me in his lap like that very first time and guides me down over his cock, but now, I know what to do.

I ride him hard until bright sparks explode behind my eyes and I shatter in a climax so beautiful, my panting breaths turn into sobs. Gorvor's knot slides into my pussy, and he comes, roaring his release as liquid heat bursts in me.

We remain locked together, bringing each other more pleasure, and Gorvor wipes my face with his hands. My tears still seem to confuse him, but he no longer forbids me from crying. I cuddle on his chest, and he hugs me close, keeping me safe.

"This is your room now," he says, his warm breath brushing over my ear.

I stiffen, still attached to him. "You mean—you don't want me to stay with you any longer?"

I'd thought we'd just reconnected. Now he's telling me to move all the way up here?

"No." He grasps my shoulders and pushes me back slightly to look me in the eyes. "You sleep in my bed. Every night. But if you need...a little time for yourself. Or if you want an office? You can do it here."

"Oh!" I look around the space with new eyes, thinking of how I could make it mine. "Thank you."

He drops his forehead to touch mine. "I would have you by my side always, little mate. But that would be too dangerous for you. So this..." He indicates the open window and the sunshine streaming in. "This is a compromise. For now. Until we can get rid of the Boar Clan and resume our normal life. Will that work for you?"

I nod eagerly. I'm already imagining flowerpots by the window, with herbs growing throughout the spring and summer months. And in the winter, I could come up here to curl up by the fire and read, or maybe knit.

"Your guards will bring you here whenever you want," he adds. "You will be safe here."

I gasp as the knot dislodges from me, and we move to the stream of water to clean up. I watch Gorvor tie the laces on his leather pants and I bite my lip, already hungry for more.

"Will you join me here?" I ask. "When you can, I mean. It can be...our hideaway."

He brushes my hair back from my face. "I would like that very much."

The warm glow in my chest expands, pulsing brightly. It's the mate bond, healthy and thriving again. The sex helped with it, of course, but it's more than that. Gorvor has shown me trust, and that's what has me grinning broadly at him. I cannot imagine what his life must have been like before he and his new clan left the old orc kingdom, but I'm so happy he did.

Now I also understand what Steagor tried to tell me—Gorvor saved them all by moving into this territory, and it's no wonder they're devoted to him. He gave them a new life, a new chance at happiness.

And he has done the same for me.

I take his hand and squeeze his fingers. "I love you."

He stops, his entire body freezing in place. Only his dark gaze darts over my face, as if he's trying to determine whether I'm telling the truth.

So I step closer and lift my other hand to his cheek. "I love you," I repeat.

He releases a pent-up breath and leans down to kiss me. His tongue strokes deep, masterfully fanning the embers of passion still smoldering inside me.

But after a moment, he tears himself away. "I would stay here with you all day and fuck you until neither of us could walk, but I wanted to show you something else," he growls. "And I love you, too, Dawn. Never doubt that."

I flush in delight, warmth rushing to my cheeks. "I thought you only wanted me because of the mate bond."

He shakes his head, and his black braid falls over his shoulder. "That was just the fertile ground, ready for our love to grow on. Being someone's mate doesn't guarantee a happy union."

Knowing he must be thinking about his parents, I wrap my arms around him and hug him tight. "Then I'm happy we found each other."

He embraces me, then tugs my hand lightly to get me going. He supports me on our way down the winding stair-case and holds my lantern for me as we walk through the warren of hallways. We surprise a couple in a darkened alcove, the male fucking his partner against the wall, but they don't seem to mind, their moans of pleasure growing louder and louder.

I stifle a giggle with my hand, and Gorvor pulls me on, chuckling darkly.

"Do you like the idea of getting caught, Dawn?" he murmurs in my ear.

A shiver runs through me at the thought.

"No?" I reply, but I sound uncertain enough that I don't even fool myself.

"Hmm." He runs his hand down my back to my ass. "We'll see if we can explore that sometime. But first..."

He motions forward, and I realize a glow is coming from behind the bend in the tunnel. The light from my lantern slowly merges with the pool of flickering torchlight, and in another couple of steps, four orcs come into view.

They're standing in front of a heavy iron portcullis, the black bars as thick as my forearm. They stand relaxed, conversing with each other, but at our approach, they straighten and hail their king.

"Dawn, you already know Bogur," Gorvor says, indicating the scout.

I knew that the orcs often changed positions inside the Hill, moving from guard duty to hunting party and back, but I've been seeing Bogur a lot lately. He must be one of Gorvor's best clan members, given how much work he does. For a moment, his cool gaze seems almost unfriendly, but he smiles and nods at me, and I shake off the strange feeling.

"And these are Uram, Korr, and Shanir," my mate goes on. "Warriors, this is Dawn, my mate."

They all bow in unison, and the one called Korr steps forward, placing his hand on his heart. "Welcome, my queen."

I raise my lantern a little higher, illuminating his serious face. "Oh, I remember you. I saw you trying to beg more honey cakes from the cook."

The males laugh, their voices echoing in the corridor.

"And you never shared with us?" Uram taunts his friend.

I lift my hand in a placating gesture. "I said he *tried* to get the cakes, not that he succeeded."

Gorvor snorts and slings his arm around my shoulders once more. "I have brought Dawn here to show her the Heart of the Hill. The gate, warriors."

Gorvor's solemn words have me itching with curiosity. Whatever lies beyond this gate must be important. The four guards and the heavy iron bars must mean that whatever is in here is either dangerous or valuable—or both.

The orcs take up their places at the large levers on either side of the gate. They strain to turn the wheels, pulling on them with all their might, and the portcullis shudders, lifting an inch. Then Gorvor steps forward and fits a huge iron key into a lock in the middle of the gate, turning it twice. Only then do the bars slide up and into the ceiling of the tunnel.

Four guards are stationed here, yet five males are needed to open it—and only Gorvor has the key. The added layer of protection surprises me. What could possibly be so important that even the guards don't have free access to it?

Gorvor takes my hand, and we slip past the guards before the portcullis is raised entirely. I duck my head and wave goodbye to the warriors, who look grateful that they don't have to raise the massive gate all the way. They strain to lower it slowly, and it settles back in place with a series of loud metallic clangs.

"We will be leaving through the other door," Gorvor

informs the guards and twists the key in the lock from the inside.

In the distance, I can just make out the end of the corridor, where it must open into a room of some sort, but I can't see what it is all the way from here. This likely means the portcullis was put in this place for a reason, too—to prevent anyone from spying on whatever is going on inside.

Apprehension rises inside me as we start down that last hallway. Tales of dragons and their mountain hoards come to mind, stories I'd listened to throughout my life, first from my grandmother before she passed away, then from traveling bards in the taverns I worked at.

But the scene that greets me at the end of the tunnel brings all those tales to shame.

We enter a cavern that's too large to have been made by human—or orc—hands. It's a natural formation, with big stalactites hanging from the ceiling and water dripping everywhere. And through it all, a massive gold vein several feet wide runs from ceiling to floor, bisecting the cave. In the torchlight, it glimmers yellow, a rich, buttery tone I've so rarely seen up close. Several orcs work on extracting the ore from the surrounding rock, the sound of their hammers and chisels ringing through the space.

The Heart of the Hill.

"We found it a year after we moved into the Hill," Gorvor says quietly from behind me. "A group of young orcs was exploring the unused tunnels, and they discovered this. There are two tunnels leading up to it—the one we came through and another that starts near the school."

I tear my gaze away from the miners and turn to him. "It was just here? Abandoned?"

He dips his chin down in a nod. "Whoever dug up this place must have found the vein. And maybe that was their downfall. Maybe they fought over it. In any case, it was forgotten."

Unable to stop myself, I glance back at the gold embedded in the wall, the ceiling, the floor. "And it won't run out?"

Gorvor lifts one shoulder in a shrug. "We've been digging it up for years. There's no sign that we're depleting the source. We've barely made a dent. And we only dig up as much as we need—because there are things more important than gold in this Hill."

That stops me from ogling all the riches surrounding us. "You mean your clan?"

He lets out a long breath. "They left the only life they knew to follow me here. I have to think of them first. We're a simple people. We were so content even before we found this. So now, I don't want to break that—or give anyone from the outside cause to attack us because of it."

"Oh," I gasp. "Is that why Charan is here?"

"We hope not," Gorvor says, grimacing. "But spending money on slaves and supporting the humans' efforts to end slavery has not gone unnoticed. Like you, others have begun to wonder how we can afford it."

"And if the Boar Clan learned about this place...?"

Gorvor looks down at me, his expression grim. "Then nothing would stop my father from crossing the human lands and attacking us. He would deem the loss of orc and human lives a good trade for the wealth he would own if he won the battle."

I glance back at the gold. With it, they could buy the entire city of Ultrup, not only the slaves at the auction. A question springs to mind, and I answer it on my own, already knowing what Gorvor will say, but I have to voice it anyway.

"Is this why you don't buy all the slaves at the barracks?" I ask. "Because you can't be seen throwing around that much coin?"

Gorvor's face grows sad. "Every time my warriors go to the auction, they are faced with the ugly task of only picking slaves who need to be rescued right then. Children. Young people who would be sold to brothels or worse." He lets out a tired sigh. "If I could, I would save them all. But then others would come and attack us, and we would not be able to protect the ones we have already saved—or our own clan."

It's an impossible conundrum, and I see the strain it causes him. I wrap my arms around his waist and lean my head on his chest.

"You will succeed," I murmur. "I know it. You are the best male I've ever met."

SEVENTEEN

Mara, for one, was overjoyed that I was finally in on the family secret and that she could now talk to me freely. With tears in her eyes, she apologized for keeping things from me, and I hugged her fiercely, apologizing in turn for being impatient and forcing her into a difficult situation.

The kitchen staff was sorry to see me drop my double shifts at the chopping board, so I agreed to continue working there whenever Mara didn't need me. With my newfound debt-free life and a mate richer than my wildest dreams, I didn't need to work, but I liked the orcs in the steamy kitchen, and it gave me an excuse to chat with the maids.

Every afternoon, I asked Vark or Steagor to take me up to the Sun Room, as we'd dubbed it, and I set up a small windowsill garden with basil, rosemary, and thyme growing in clay pots. Gorvor brought me some wildflower seeds from his next hunt, but I saved them for the next growing season when I could sow them in the early spring. As summer bloomed to its full extent, we turned the small room into a cozy sanctuary where Gorvor joined me most days for an hour or more of lovemaking and well-earned rest.

On a rainy morning, Gorvor and I are enjoying breakfast at our table in the great hall, when Bogur arrives, soaked through but grinning. He approaches the king and murmurs into his ear. Whatever news the scout has brought seems to be intended for Gorvor first, so I sit as patiently as possible, munching on a ripe, juicy peach, and curb my curiosity.

I'll find out what's going on sooner or later. My mate doesn't keep secrets from me anymore.

Gorvor stands, then bends down to kiss me on the lips. "I will return shortly, Dawn."

I follow him with my gaze as he disappears through the kitchen door, then focus on the scout.

"Will you join me?" I ask, indicating the hearty breakfast spread on the table in front of me.

Bogur gives me a slight bow, and he brings up a chair and tucks in, his hunger apparent.

I let the poor male get a couple of bites in, then ask, "Can you tell me the news you've brought?"

His gaze darts around the room, and he lowers his voice. "I was watching the northern mountain pass. And I spotted a herd of mountain sheep grazing in a meadow."

He says this as if it should mean something to me, almost buzzing with excitement.

"And that's...good?" I venture.

He nods eagerly. "Their wool is pure white, so it's extremely valuable. And the meat is a delicacy we don't often get to eat. The herd was large, so we could easily harvest several animals without hurting it."

"That's wonderful," I say. "Will you go after them?"

"If the king allows it," he replies.

It's clear to me what he would choose if the decision was up to him. I let the scout return to his breakfast and take a sip of tea. I should talk to Gorvor soon. If his people have to trudge through heavy rain to hunt for sheep, maybe he is being a little too careful with the gold. I understand trying to preserve an appearance of a modest life for his clan, but if his orcs are living on top of an actual gold mine, they should partake in the abundance, too. The king included. Gorvor has had to take care of everyone for so long, I wonder if anyone ever took care of him.

But this is not the time to question his decisions. He returns moments later and claps the scout on his back.

Then he turns to the crowded dining hall and calls, "Hunters, we gather at the gate in a quarter hour. We will feast tonight."

A cheer goes up from the long tables, and a baby bursts into a fit of crying, startled by the noise. His father soothes him quickly, then hands him off to his mate and kisses her soundly. Throughout the hall, hunters rise from their seats and leave for their quarters to gather their longbows.

I grasp Gorvor's hand before he can leave, too. "I have a suggestion if you'll take it."

He raises his eyebrows but sits back on his carved wooden throne, gaze intent on me. I love how he focuses all his attention when I speak and doesn't brush me away. "Tell me."

I whisper, "I think you should invite Charan to hunt with you."

His expression hardens. "Why would I do that?"

I reach for him and rub my thumb over the fierce divot between his furrowed eyebrows. "Because I think it would help your relationship. He is here to make sure you're not going to try and threaten his rule when your father dies.

Maybe this is a good time to reassure him that you have no intention of taking that crown? Especially as you'll be hunting sheep today, not boar?"

I give him a significant look, and he laughs, mollified.

"Very well, little mate. Your suggestion is wise. I will ask him."

He leans in for another kiss and leaves me, his long legs carrying him across the hall to where Charan and his men are sitting at a separate table. Even from the distance, I can see the surprise on Charan's face when his brother invites him along. The other three orcs shake their heads despite Charan urging them on. One motions toward the door, as if to indicate the horrible weather. But their leader seems determined to join in on the hunt. He gets up and leaves, presumably to get his weapons, too, and Gorvor strides for the corridor that leads to our bedroom.

I remain in my seat, sipping my tea and watching the rest of Charan's group. They huddle close together, their heads almost touching. I wish I could be a fly on the wall to listen in on their conversation—I didn't miss the flash of displeasure that shot across the face of the big warrior who's sitting facing me when Gorvor stepped up to their table. Now, they don't look too happy that their leader has decided to hunt with the Black Bear Clan.

Most of all, I'm surprised at the fact that the three remaining Boar Clan orcs are staying here. I would have thought that they'd want to provide some sort of security for their chief, but they remain at the table, scowling at anyone who passes too close to them. The Black Bear Clan orcs avoid them as much as they can, and a strange sort of bubble forms around the strangers' table, as if they are a rock in a river of orcs flowing around them.

I wave goodbye to the hunters when they leave through

the front door, then take up my work with Mara, helping her answer correspondence and order supplies for the coming months. Neekar and Ozork will be traveling to the city soon, and I want them to start establishing relationships with the women's clothes merchants in Ultrup in advance of my first shipment of ladies' products.

After lunch, I ask Vark and Steagor to accompany me to the Sun Room—I have to water the plants and sweep the floor, and I'm hoping that Gorvor might find me there if he returns from the hunt soon enough.

I've even become used to the spiral staircase that leads up to my little haven, but today, my lantern flickers sadly on the way up, the flame shortening and slowly dimming.

"Take my hand," Vark says as darkness closes in around us.

I put my palm on the wall, supporting myself. "It's fine, I'll manage. It's just a few more steps."

Peering at the lantern, I shake it gently. I could have sworn I'd added oil to it recently, but I've had so many things to do, it's possible it had slipped my mind.

"The king will use our guts as festival ornaments if you trip and break your neck," Steagor mutters from behind me.

"Then it's good you'll catch me before I fall," I say, resolutely trudging on.

Vark lets out a snort. "You are a fine queen for Gorvor."

I pause, catching my breath. "How do you figure that?"

I secretly agree with him, of course. I'm the perfect queen for Gorvor because he's my mate. It took me a while, but I have accepted my role, and I wouldn't trade it for the world.

"You don't back down," he says. "Even on your first day here, you screamed at us for letting him take you into his room."

I glower at his back. "I still haven't entirely forgiven you for that, you know."

"Ah, we knew he wouldn't hurt you," Vark says. "That's not the kind of male he is."

"Besides," Steagor adds, his voice a rumble in the dark. "You wouldn't have believed us."

I open my mouth to object, then close it again. He's not wrong.

"I'm sorry," I say. "I came here with a lot of prejudice."

Steagor surprises me with a laugh. "It's all right, my lady."

We reach the top, and I unlock the door with the key Gorvor has given me. Light floods into the corridor, and I squint and shade my eyes at the sudden brightness. I'd left the shutters cracked open for the plants, and even though the day is gloomy, my eyes sting for a moment before they adjust.

"Oh, no," I cry, springing forward. "What a mess!"

The shutters, while letting in the light, also let in a flood of rain, and now the stone floor is wet, the curtains are soaked, and my plants are half drowning in their pots.

"I will get you more lamp oil," Steagor says from the doorway, picking up my discarded lantern. "I will return shortly."

Vark scoffs at him. "You just want to avoid helping with the cleaning."

The older orc shrugs and departs, leaving us in the Sun Room. Vark grumbles as he works, but he helps me mop up the worst of the puddles, then lifts the heavy soil-filled flowerpots and pours the excess water off through the window.

I'm on my knees, wiping the flagstones yet again, when Vark suddenly straightens and turns toward the door.

"Be quiet," he says urgently.

I stop mid-swipe and strain my ears. I can't hear anything, but Vark's entire posture changes. He drops into his fighter's stance and pulls a long knife from his weapons belt with one hand and a short hatchet with the other.

"What is it?" I whisper.

"Orcs coming up the stairs. Could be nothing, but it's not Steagor, and our people know this is your private room." He walks to the threshold and glances back at me. "You will be safe in here. Do not open the door until I tell you, do you understand? Lock yourself in and secure the bolt."

I nod, shivering. "Why can't you stay in here and wait with me? You'd be safe in here as well."

The look he gives me could freeze water. "I'm an orc. I do not hide. And Steagor will soon return. He could walk into an ambush."

I want to object—orcs can be hurt as much as humans —but this is what he does. What he has trained for all his life. I squeeze my hands into fists and nod, refraining from arguing with him.

Even I can hear the rattle of steel now. Whoever is coming up the long staircase has come prepared for battle.

"Do it now," Vark snaps. "Lock. Bolt. Do not open the door unless it's me or Steagor on the other side."

With shaking hands, I obey his order. He steps into the short corridor, his weapons at the ready, and I slam the door behind him, feeling sick to my stomach. I fit the key into the lock and turn it twice, then slide the heavy iron bolt across, securing myself inside. Helplessness threatens to overwhelm me. This room, so remote and private, has been such a joy to use, but now it has become a prison—and Vark is out there, risking his life for me.

I have to help him somehow.

I run to the window and scream into the rain, "Help! We're being attacked in the Sun Room! Help us!"

No answer comes, and the relentless patter of the falling raindrops smothers my voice. We're so high up and so far away from any of the guarded entrances to the Hill that even on a nice day, it would be a stretch to call for help from here. Now, I have no chance of being heard. I look toward the top of the cliff that the window is cut from, then down, trying to see if I can find a way out of here and warn someone. But the sheer rock wall would be too dangerous to scale even in dry weather. I would fall and break my neck before I could ever get to safety.

From the other side of the thick oakwood door, shouts catch my attention. I run back to the entrance and press my ear to the wood.

"We're here for the girl," a rough voice states. "You don't have to die."

"Piss off." Vark's voice is easily recognizable, cold with fury. "I'll kill you all and let your bodies rot."

Of course, my mind paints the image of the culprits clearly. The Boar Clan orcs. They likely realized that with the king and most of the warriors gone from the Hill, this was their perfect chance to attack.

At the first clash of steel, I jump back, terrified. Grunts and shouts fill the space, muffled and yet too close. Panic rises inside me. However many assailants came up those stairs, Vark is out there alone, likely outnumbered. And even if he's the better warrior, this is a numbers game—how long will it take them to wear him down? The close quarters of the corridor make it hard for more than one soldier to jump him at a time, so that will buy him time. So will the short-range weapons he always carries on his belt. But if one slips past him...

Maybe I could open the door quickly and stab whoever is close enough to reach? I search the room frantically for any sort of weapon, but we didn't design this space to hold an arsenal. The best I can come up with is one of Gorvor's short-bladed knives for sharpening the writing quills. Its blade is barely as long as my thumb, but it's sharp and handy for me to hold, unlike the large knives the orcs use for battle or hunting.

Clutching the little weapon, I return to the door, only to realize my mistake. Any sneak attack on my part would have to be sudden and silent, and there is no way I could both unbolt and unlock the door without giving myself away to the combatants outside. I would only distract Vark and get him killed faster.

I wish Steagor would return, but to fetch the lamp oil and walk all the way back here, it will take him a while. The attackers timed this right.

A grunt of pain has me flinching, even though I don't know who it is. The idea that males are fighting outside my door because of me is so abhorrent, my hands tremble uncontrollably. I nearly drop the knife at the thought of someone getting killed.

But I force myself to think of Gorvor. What would he have me do? He would say I needed to fight. To make the best of a bad situation and make sure I survive.

Gorvor.

It could be hours yet before he returns. I wonder what he will find when he seeks me out. Because I'm sure he will. If I'm not in our bedroom, waiting for him, he will come up here to search for me. I only have to hold out that long. In the meantime, Steagor will bring back the lantern, and maybe he can help defeat the attackers.

But another pained sound comes from the other side of the door, and then, two loud knocks. I jump back, staring at the lock as if it might bite me. Only Gorvor and I have the keys to this room, so nobody can get in by unlocking it, but there are other ways. They could break down the door. It would take them a while, because it's sturdy and reinforced with iron, but orcs are nothing if not strong.

"Open the door, girl," a rough voice calls through the wood. "Or your filthy little guard dies."

My breath lodges in my throat. I can't answer. Vark said not to open the door for anyone but him or Steagor, but if he's not the one speaking, he must be...

My mind rebels at the thought. No. The orc said they will kill Vark if I don't comply, so he must be alive. Or the stranger is lying, which is exactly what I would expect him to do.

"I will count to ten," the male snarls as if impatience is getting the best of him. "If you don't unlock this door by then, I will slit his throat, and his death will be on you."

I sob in terror, my heart hammering wildly. If I don't open the door, Vark will die. I know it as surely as I know my name. They will not let a witness live. But maybe if I go with them willingly, they'll let him live. I could trade myself in for a chance to save his life—I'm clearly what they're after, so there's a chance they want me alive.

"Four," the male calls, counting off slowly. "Three."

I can't let him die.

Gritting my teeth, I put my weight into pushing the bolt open. The orc outside stops counting, and silence descends as if he's waiting for me to make the final decision. I fit the key back in the lock, take a deep breath, and turn it twice,.

quickly. Then, rather than open the door myself, I dance back and stand in the far corner of the small room.

Something slams against the door, and it flies open, cracking loudly on the stone wall. Then an orc strides in, a big male with broad shoulders and a chest plate and helmet made of polished steel. It's one of Charan's companions, as I suspected. Behind him in the corridor lie three orcs—one is Vark, his body crumpled on the floor, and the other two are two more Boar Clan orcs.

The only male left standing faces off with me. He's bleeding from his leg and he seems to be missing two fingers on his left hand, but it's his scowl that's the most terrifying. He looks like he wants to murder me right where I stand.

"Come."

He makes as if he wants to grab me by the waist, but I jump aside just in time—and press the small knife to my neck.

"Don't come any closer," I yelp, my hand shaking but my grip firm.

He stops and straightens, a calculating expression crossing his face. "What are you doing?"

I angle the knife so he can see it better and point at Vark with my free hand. "I will only come with you if you let him live."

EIGHTEEN

I squint, trying to take stock of my guard's injuries. A sickening red wound gapes on his forehead, spreading blood everywhere. I know all head wounds bleed copiously, but this is too much. The foul smell of spilled intestines, coming from one of the attackers, wafts into the room. I focus back on the soldier in front of me and swallow, hoping I won't be sick.

"I'll only go with you if you let me bandage his wounds," I insist. "He's going to die otherwise."

"Give me the knife," the orc snarls, lunging for me again. "I meant to take you alive, but there's no need for you to stay intact."

Bile rises in my throat, and I fight to keep my thoughts steady. "No. You come any closer, and I'll slit my own throat. Then you'll be out two men *and* your prize. Your leader won't be happy with you if I die."

I'm taking a massive gamble with this. If I'm too much trouble for him, there will come a moment when he decides I'm not worth it. That's when my life will be forfeit, and I won't be able to help Vark either.

The orc scowls at me, then retreats a step. "Fine. Hurry. But you're wasting your time. He's as good as dead."

I could sob with relief but I don't want to give him the option to grab me while my attention is elsewhere.

I straighten my shoulders and try to make my voice as queenly as possible. "Go stand on the lower landing. If I so much as see you move toward me, our deal is off."

He grunts but complies, moving four steps down the staircase. He keeps his gaze on me, his hands at his hips. I could use his help shifting Vark's heavy body into a better position, but I guess I'll have to bandage him where he lies half slumped against the wall.

Darting back into the room, I tear the sheet off the bed and rip it into strips of linen. Then I have to put down the knife to bandage Vark's head, but I keep it close, ready in case the attacker chooses to change his mind. He huffs and shuffles his feet, though, and stays where he is. The one thing keeping me and my guard alive right now is the fact that this orc thinks I have the upper hand. I don't. My only defenses are my quick reflexes and my ability to bluff my way through life.

Would I slit my throat if he came at me? I have no idea how to answer that question. I simply hope it won't come to that.

Vark's wound is still bleeding copiously when I press a wadded-up piece of linen to it and tie another tightly around his head. If his chest wasn't moving with slow, shallow breaths, I'd think he was dead. My stomach revolts again, threatening to eliminate everything I ate today, but I force myself to stay calm. Even if Vark survives, he will likely lose his left eye. The cut goes deep, ruining his cheek, his eyelid, and his forehead. I cover it up as best I can and pray to the gods that Steagor returns soon—if not to rescue me, then to help Vark get the help he needs.

It's still a long shot. In the human world, such injuries would most likely be fatal. But here...if there's still magic in the orc realm, maybe Vark will stand a chance.

I use another strip of linen to bandage the brutal wound in my guard's thigh, cinching the knot tight to stop the flow of blood. He has minor scrapes and cuts all over, but those will have to wait—the orc on the stairs is becoming impatient.

"Come on," he says. "There's nothing more you can do for him."

I pick up my little knife, stand, and wipe my bloody hands on my dress. I try not to look at the other two orcs lying in the corridor. Their blood pools on the cold stone floor, already congealing in a sticky mess, and the entrails of the one who Vark gutted are strewn over his legs where he fell to the floor. I lift my skirts and step over the corpses, but the scent of the refuse overwhelms me.

I double over just in time to be sick. My tears flow freely as I heave painfully, and by the time the last orc standing walks over to me and disarms me with a casual gesture, I'm too weakened to even protest. His foul curses ring through the stairwell. He picks me up and slings me over his shoulder.

"Filthy human," he snarls. "You disgust me."

I choke and cough, my stomach pressed uncomfortably over his shoulder. My hair falls all over my face, and I'm so disoriented by the dark, I soon lose track of where we are. I don't know how the orc manages to get all the twists and turns in the corridors right, but we never backtrack. Once, he dumps me roughly to the floor, then picks me up and holds a knife to my throat, his big, calloused palm covering my mouth.

I don't even hear the footsteps in the dark until they're right on top of us, but I don't dare cry out. Muffled as my scream might have been, whoever is passing would hear me, but I can't be sure it's a warrior. Even if I somehow survive, the other orc could be killed, and I don't want any more blood on my hands.

The moment the footsteps recede, we're on our way again. My head hurts from being turned upside down, and I know I'll be bruised all over after this. Not that it will matter. I can't see a future in which this turns out well for me. I try to hold back my sobs and just hang on, but it's becoming increasingly clear that this orc knows very well how to evade the Black Bear Clan guards. We enter what seems like a very wet, dank tunnel, but I realize quickly it's the sewer system, where the refuse from all the bathrooms in the Hill is being washed away by the underground stream.

The only unguarded exit from the Hill.

We come out smelling bad even to my less sensitive nose, and the big orc keeps up a steady stream of curses as he lopes off into the rain-soaked forest. At one point, he changes his grip on me, holding me in his arms in front of him in a travesty of a gentle hug.

I wish I still had my little quill sharpener so I could stick it in his neck.

I try to make myself as unpleasant to carry as possible. I wiggle and hit his chin with my elbow, I yell and scratch and scream. I persist until he puts me down on the muddy forest ground beside a stream and backhands me across the face with so much force, I topple off my feet and slam into the trunk of a fir tree.

Eyes watering, I palm my stinging face and run my tongue along my teeth to see if he knocked any out. There's a bloody cut on the inside of my cheek, filling my mouth with a coppery taste, and I retch again, thinking of all the blood that was spilled today.

Then I spit on the ground, spraying the orc's heavy boots with droplets of bloody saliva. "Gorvor will kill you for this."

The orc snorts. "Your king is weak. He couldn't even protect his mate. Now be quiet and get in the water or I'll repeat what I just did for as long as I have to."

I sink into sullen silence but obey his order. I wash the stink of the sewers from my body as best I can and scrub my hands to wash away the blood. The orc does the same, grunting at the chilly water. By the time I stumble back onto the bank, my dress is soaked through and heavy with water, and I'm shivering uncontrollably from the cold. The orc picks me up again and resumes running. It takes us a long while to reach a small forest clearing, and by that time, I'm so tired, my eyelids are drooping from exhaustion.

Unconsciousness seems like a good idea, but I can't fall asleep. I want to know everything that's going on—and if an opportunity comes along for me to escape, I need to be lucid enough to take it.

When two shapes detach themselves from the lush greenery, my heart skips in excitement—but my relief is short-lived.

One of the orcs greeting us with a raised hand is Charan, which comes as no surprise. He is likely the one who orchestrated the whole plan.

The other is Bogur. The orc I shared breakfast with this morning. The trusted scout who sent Gorvor and his men hunting after a flock of prized sheep that probably don't even exist.

"Where are Sarr and Trubor?" Charan asks, his forehead creasing in a frown.

The orc carrying me dumps me on the ground. I land on my butt in the wet grass and tumble to my side, then pick myself up on shaking legs.

"They're dead," my abductor snarls. "Her guard killed them."

He lifts his hand again, moving to strike me, but Charan jumps between us and catches his arm before the blow lands.

"Are you mad?" Gorvor's brother snarls at his soldier. "This is insane. We need to return the queen. The king will kill us all if he—"

An arrow whistles through the air and hits the orc who kidnapped me between the eyes. The orc jerks back and tumbles to the ground, his dead black eyes staring up at the clouds.

NINETEEN

Charan drops his soldier's arm and swivels around, then ducks just enough that the arrow aiming for his head only nicks his ear. The second arrow catches him in the thigh, passing straight through, and he stumbles but keeps upright. His hand goes to his belt where his large battle-axe hangs in a loop of leather, but he freezes before pulling it out.

It takes me a moment to realize that Charan has stopped moving, because I'm too engrossed in staring at the dead body lying on the ground. But at his sudden stillness, I squint at the bushes. From all sides of the clearing, shirtless orcs suddenly melt from the leafy undergrowth, their green skin a perfect camouflage in the dim afternoon light.

Warrior after warrior steps into the clearing, and they herd Bogur back, their longbows drawn.

And there is Gorvor, slipping from the shadows like a wraith, incorporeal one moment and imposing the next. He is nocking another arrow, and I know right then he was the one who took down my kidnapper and stopped his brother.

The tall longbow is pulled tight, a weapon meant for killing prey at large distances but just as deadly from up close.

"Dawn," he says, his voice vibrating with fury. "Step away from him."

I scurry to the side, then run toward him, drawn by my love and the mate bond, the worry that I'd never see him again and the relief that he's here, alive. But I stop several steps from him, unsure of what to do. I don't want to throw myself into his arms when he's still aiming at Charan's heart.

Then Gorvor lowers his bow and extends one arm for me. I fly to him, wrapping my arms around his waist, and he squeezes me close and buries his face in my hair.

"Are you all right?" he murmurs in my ear.

I nod against his chest, too shaken to form words.

Gorvor holds me for a long minute, and no one in the clearing moves. Finally, he releases me and looks into my face. His expression darkens, and he takes my chin gently and examines the cheek where my abductor struck me. It hurts, and I expect it to turn a magnificent shade of purple soon as my eye is already swelling shut.

"I want to kill him again," Gorvor growls.

I take a hold of his hand and press it between my palms. "He can't hurt me anymore. You've made sure of that."

He jerks his head down in a curt nod, then lets go of me. "Go wait with Neekar, little mate. I need to take care of this."

He means to kill the two captured orcs. And I could go and hide with Neekar, but I don't want to do that.

I put my hand on Gorvor's arm. "I will stay with you. But you should send someone back to the Hill. Vark was seriously injured, and I had to leave him in the corridor at the Sun Room." My chest squeezes at the thought of that scene. "I managed to bandage his wounds but I don't know if he'll make it."

He flashes me a look that conveys both pride and relief. Maybe he thought I would shrink away from him because of this. But a guard lies dying in the Hill because of these males, and I've had it with being kidnapped. I want to see justice done.

Gorvor motions to his men, and one of them rushes back into the forest, heading toward the Hill. Three warriors converge on Bogur and force him to his knees. Then they stuff his ears with torn-up cloth, drop a heavy woolen hood over his head, and turn him away from Charan and the king. I frown, wondering what's going on, and then it hits me—they want to question them separately.

The king steps closer to his brother and stares at him with unconcealed distaste. Charan tries to retreat, but when he puts his weight on his wounded leg, he hisses in pain and stops.

"Tell me," Gorvor says. "Was everything we talked about today to throw me off the scent?"

His younger brother shakes his head. "No. I meant every word."

I wonder what happened between them. Did they get a chance to discuss peace between the kingdoms? But barging in with my questions would be inappropriate right now, so I bite my tongue and wait, hoping for more information.

"Then why did you leave the hunt with Bogur?" Gorvor demands.

Charan's gaze dips to the ground. "I only learned of the plan to lure you away from the Hill when he told me on the hunt. We'd talked about using your mate to...speed along our negotiations. But I never gave the order to my men to kidnap her like this. Or to hurt her."

He looks at me, and his already ashen skin turns gray. He winces, probably at the emerging bruise on my face, then hangs his head. And despite how troublesome he's been in the past weeks, I can't sense any insincerity in Charan's voice now. He could be a very good liar—or he's telling the truth.

"What happened, then?" Gorvor taunts. "Why did they act on their own?"

The orc glowers at this, some of his color returning. "They were not *my* men. They answered to our father. He must have given them orders I knew nothing about."

Gorvor lets out an impatient sound. "What was your real purpose here, brother? To kill me?"

Charan's gaze snaps up. "No! I only wanted to make sure you wouldn't take back our father's crown."

My mate drags his hand over his face, spraying water droplets to the ground. He suddenly seems tired, as if the weight of the world is sitting on his shoulders. "How many times do I have to reject it?" he asks. "I didn't want it then, and I don't want it now. I only want my people to live in peace."

Charan nods vehemently. "All right. I will take your word for it, and we can put all of this behind us."

I don't think that's the whole truth, but I don't know how to get the full story from Charan.

Gorvor is not done with his questions, either. "What role did Bogur play in all of this?"

His brother's throat bobs as he swallows. "He approached us some time after we arrived here. He said he could help us get you out of the way. The plan to take your mate was his suggestion." His gaze darts to me again, to my swelling cheek, and back to Gorvor. "He said you would go mad without her. And he told us about the gold."

One of the warriors lets out a foul curse, and the resolve on Gorvor's face hardens. This is the secret they've all been protecting, sometimes at great cost. And if Charan knows it, he could spread the word throughout his own kingdom—and bring an army here to wrest the Hill away from the Black Bear Clan.

"I don't want your gold, brother," Charan says quickly. "When I am king, I will change things in the Boar Clan territory."

He sounds so sincere, I want to believe him. If this could be resolved without more bloodshed, I want it to work out, but I'm not sure what to think. To put the fate of our entire clan in the hands of one male who has already proven himself to be a conniving enemy...it would be foolish.

Gorvor doesn't reply. I don't know what he's thinking, and apparently neither does Charan, because he's getting more and more agitated, shuffling his weight from foot to foot, then wincing and favoring his wounded leg. A trickle of blood from his pierced ear is washed away by the rain, until only a thin rivulet of pink runs over his grayish-green skin.

But there's a definitive family resemblance between him and Gorvor, in the shape of their eyes and their build. I wonder if Gorvor sees it, too—and if he's hesitating because of it.

Finally, the king motions for his warriors to remove the hood from Bogur's head and the cloth from his ears. They muffle Charan's hearing this time and drop the hood over his eyes, and he sways slightly, as if disoriented. Two of the warriors grab him by the arms and ease him to the ground. The hood bobs, and Charan murmurs a word of thanks, then extends his wounded leg in front of him.

I focus my attention on the scout who sat at my table in the great hall just this morning and calmly told me about the sheep they were supposed to hunt. He shakes his head and sneers at me, then fixes a baleful glare on Gorvor.

The king's gaze is sad when he approaches his warrior. And I know that even though Charan is his brother, this betrayal hurts him more. His people were the ones who followed him away from the old kingdom into a better life, and he thinks of them as his family. Now this male has plunged a dagger straight into that trust and ruined it.

"Why?" Gorvor asks simply.

The male moves his knees farther apart as if bracing himself on the ground. "We have enough gold to gild the whole Hill, and you have us running around the forest, chasing goats." He spits the words out with rage, his gaze cold.

And it hits me—he resents having to work if his clan has so much wealth.

To my surprise, one of the other warriors steps forward, a hunter I've never been introduced to. "We all decided to keep the gold a secret. To use it only as needed. You voted the same, Bogur."

I lift my eyebrows at this. I had no idea Gorvor had put the decision to a vote, but knowing him, it makes sense. He wanted the best for his people, and if they had decided to live a different life, he would have given it to them.

The king motions to his warrior, and the male falls back with a small bow. Then Gorvor turns back to the traitor. "You could have come to me if you were displeased. We all chose to work hard and preserve the mine for our children.

Instead, you betrayed us to our enemies. You endangered my mate."

His voice deepens to a growl, and a flicker of fury passes over his face as he says this, showing for the first time how tenuous his control is. He's angry, yet he is holding back to pass fair judgment.

Bogur's sneer is so different from the friendly smile he offered me this morning. "She's just a human."

"She is your queen," Gorvor roars.

Silence descends on the clearing, with only the rustle of the raindrops falling on leaves disturbing the quiet. A vein throbs in the king's neck, and he grips the head of the battle-axe at his waist.

Bogur's chin juts out. "I do not recognize her as my queen. When I followed you here, you promised us a better life." He spits on the ground in front of Gorvor. "Here's what I think of that."

Gorvor has once more regained composure, and he regards Bogur with disgust. "Did Charan approach you when he came here?"

The kneeling male shakes his head. "He isn't fit to rule. The future king should be able to make hard decisions. He doesn't have the stomach for it."

"So you made the plan to kidnap Dawn?" the king presses.

I wonder why he's asking all this when Charan has already told us, but then it hits me—he's trying to see if Charan was telling us the truth.

"My plan was to have her killed," Bogur answers, his voice cold. "The pain of losing your mate would have either killed you or driven you insane, and the Hill would have been an easy target. I separated her guards and gave these fools every opportunity, but they didn't deliver her head like I'd asked."

The knowledge that I came this close to dying sends a shiver through me. If Charan didn't order the kill and Bogur wanted me dead—then I'm only alive because the orc who kidnapped me either thought I was more useful to him alive or he found a spark of pity for me. I can guess which one is more likely.

The way Bogur leaves nothing out, easily incriminating himself, tells me that he already knows what his sentence will be. But I still cringe back when Gorvor pulls the heavy axe from his weapons belt.

I thought he might give the order to one of his warriors, but he takes up a solid stance in front of the kneeling male and lifts the axe high.

Bogur looks at the sky, his arms still bound behind his back. Rain pelts on his face, and for a moment, he seems almost peaceful. Then his face twists with rage again, and he lets out a string of foul curses, abusing Gorvor and everyone who chooses to follow him.

The stream of filth is cut off by a single, powerful strike of the king's axe.

Bogur's head lands on the grass and rolls to the side, stopping facedown by a clump of late-summer oxeye daisies. The stump of the male's neck pumps blood for several seconds, then topples over in a bloody heap.

I gasp and turn away, the image already stuck in my mind. I knew it was going to happen, yet it doesn't make the horror any easier to bear. Then I take a deep breath through my mouth to avoid smelling the blood and face Gorvor again.

He is crouched by the body, cleaning off his axe on the dead male's tunic. He stands slowly and hooks the weapon back through its loop. His expression is guarded, as if he thinks I might not want to touch him now he has executed one of his warriors. I step toward him, tentative, not sure if he wants me to hug and kiss him in front of his people. But the moment I move, he springs forward, wraps me in his arms, and lifts me off my feet.

He buries his face in my hair and squeezes me so hard, I let out an *oof* of surprise.

"I'm all right," I murmur in his ear as I stroke his wet black hair. "I'm alive."

"If I wasn't here to stop them, only the gods know what might have happened." He shudders, his shoulders shaking. "Forgive me. I didn't protect you well enough."

I frown and pinch his arm. I don't believe it hurts him, but he looks at me with anguished, dark eyes.

"Don't shame your warriors by saying I wasn't well protected," I growl. "Vark killed two males and injured one more, and Steagor only left us because we were safe in the Sun—"

I cut myself off, remembering Bogur's last words. He claimed he purposefully separated my guards, so...

"Oh," I gasp. "He must have tampered with my lantern. And Steagor went to fill it with more oil, which was when the Boar Clan orcs attacked."

Another shudder passes through me at the idea of him watching me closely enough to know that I needed that lantern. To know where I would be the most vulnerable.

Gorvor's nostrils flare. "His plan exposed weaknesses we cannot afford to have. How did they get you out of the Hill?"

I wrinkle my nose. "Through the sewers."

At a flick of the king's fingers, two more warriors separate themselves from the group and disappear into the forest, likely headed to secure that exit. I don't envy them their job—the smell alone will make this the least desirable of all guard posts in the Hill.

"How did you know where to find us?" I ask Gorvor, looping my arms around his neck.

He scowls. "Charan and Bogur disappeared from the hunting party. In the rain, it took us a while to find the spot where they'd left the path and backtracked through the forest. Bogur knew the way well. But when we knew what to look for, we could travel faster."

I press a kiss to his cheek. "Thank you for finding me in time. But I don't understand why Bogur hated this life so much if he chose it. He left the Boar Clan with you of his own volition, didn't he?"

"He did." My mate lets out a long sigh. "I think he hoped for a better position in the new clan. Back in the old kingdom, he was the youngest son of one of my father's generals. His family enjoyed a lot of the...privileges my father handed out to his closest followers. But on his own, he didn't have much wealth."

The way he says *privileges* tells me I don't want to ask about the specifics.

"And here he had to actually work to earn a living," I guess. "Which bothered him even more."

"I had no idea he was this unhappy," Gorvor admits quietly.

I fix him with a stern look. "This is not on you. His actions are not your fault. Ask any of your other warriors, and they will tell you they are happy."

"It's true," Neekar pipes up from behind me. "We are."

"And you shouldn't be eavesdropping," Gorvor growls at him, but there's no heat in his words.

I hide my smile by kissing my mate's cheek again, and

he lets out a hum I interpret as a sign of contentment. He finally lets me go, and within minutes, he dispatches four males to dig a hole for Bogur's body—he will not get the honor of being burned on a pyre in a warrior's funeral— and two more tie a makeshift bandage around Charan's leg and help him to his feet. In a slow procession, we head toward the settlement, the rain obliterating our muddy tracks.

I take no more than three unsteady steps before Gorvor swings me up in his arms again and nestles me against his chest.

"I have nothing dry to wrap you in," he mutters in dismay, "but I can give you my own warmth."

"Thank you." I press my chilled hands to his skin. "What will happen to Charan?"

He sighs deeply. "I don't know yet. For now, we will patch him up and let him recover. Then we might send him back to his kingdom, but I don't know if we can trust him to keep our secret."

"So he'll be your prisoner?" I ask.

"For now." He peers down at me. "Does that bother you?"

I shake my head. "I like the idea of keeping him somewhere we can be sure he can do no harm."

Gorvor snorts. "How vicious you are, little mate."

"When the people I love are in danger, all bets are off," I murmur and snuggle closer to him.

"Tell me again," he says, falling back a step so his words are obscured from the others by our footsteps and the patter of rain.

I look up at him. "Tell you what?"

"That you love me."

I lift my hand to his cheek and say, "I love you, Gorvor."

"I love you, too, little mate," he replies, a growl entering his voice. He picks up speed again, marching with a renewed purpose. "Now I want to get back to the Hill and make sure you're comfortable and uninjured. I might have to take off all your clothes for that."

I loop my arms around his head and pull him in for a scorching kiss that heats me up from the inside and has Gorvor stumbling a little on the uneven forest floor.

"Hurry, my lord."

EPILOGUE

Two months later, on the eve of the autumn equinox

I stand in front of the open chest that holds my dresses and look down at my bust in dismay. The silk fabric, which used to be snug but not too tight, strains over my breasts and pushes them up in a most inappropriate way.

For human standards, that is.

I'm not bothered by the fact that I'm showing more flesh than usual anymore—not since I've become used to the orc habits and have come to love my body, whether it's clothed or not. No, I'm concerned about my ability to *breathe* in this dress, noble as it is, because it's honestly constricting my lungs and my movements.

But it will have to do. I haven't had the heart to give the seamstresses we've hired an order for clothing because it seems so frivolous compared to the much more important task they've been working on—preparing our first shipment of ladies' products that will be taken to Ultrup next week.

After the mess with the Boar Clan orcs, it took Gorvor weeks to calm down enough that he allowed me to visit town. He came along, of course, leaving the Hill in Steagor's capable hands for the first time in years, and we had double the usual number of guards with us. But I visited several ladies' clothes merchants and formed new friendships with women who were astonished by the samples I'd brought with me.

From then on, the enthusiasm for my business venture has only grown, and I'm hopeful it'll become successful in the future. Gorvor has been with me every step of the way, supporting me and helping out, and has given me enough funds to get things off the ground.

But as much as I hate bothering the seamstresses in this busy time, I think I'll need to talk to them soon.

My courses are several weeks late, and I'm fairly sure I'm pregnant.

Hence the tight dress and the sensitive breasts. I don't think Gorvor has put the signs together yet—he hasn't said anything, and I think orc women might experience pregnancy a little differently. So I will tell him tonight, after the feast, which he promised will be unlike anything I've been used to so far.

In his words, this is a harvest celebration where we plant seed for the new year and thank the gods for the bounty of our fields. Orcs from the surrounding villages will join in on the celebration, and apparently, it goes on late into the night.

I place my palm on my still-flat belly. A giddy shiver passes through me. This time next year, I'll have a baby to cuddle and take care of. Our little son or daughter will be born out of love, to parents who will be overjoyed to greet a new life.

But now I am running behind, and it won't do for the queen to be late. I place the thin iron circlet that Gorvor had made for me on my head and secure it with a couple of pins. It's simple and effective—and when I stand beside Gorvor, I think we look so good together.

Hurrying to the door, I pick up my lantern and throw open the bolt. Then I pull open the door—and stop.

The corridor is lit up, a string of lanterns going in both directions from our room.

"Oh!"

My hand flies to my mouth, and I blink hard to banish the happy tears that spring up in my eyes. Gorvor must have done this. He lit up our home for me, so I won't have to carry the lantern anymore.

I find Steagor and Neekar standing at attention, splendid in their new tunics with the black bear emblem stitched into the collars. They grin at me, even serious Steagor, and I suppose I do look funny, gaping at all the pretty lights. I return their smiles, carry the lantern back into the bedroom, and start down the corridor, eager to join the king at the feast. The only thing that dims my excitement a little is my disappointment at the fact that Vark still hasn't returned to his post.

The big guard had recovered from his injuries, though the head wound had nearly taken his life. Steagor had found him in that corridor and carried him down the steep staircase, bellowing for help, until other orcs heard him and helped him lug Vark's heavy body to the infirmary. There, Vark had fought for his life as an infection had set in, and he'd barely made it through.

He'd lost his left eye, and he'd taken the injury hard. Ever since he left the infirmary a couple of weeks ago, he has been resting and recovering his strength, and every time Gorvor has asked him whether he was ready to resume his guard duties, he has asked for more time. I'd tried to talk to him, but he has been avoiding me. I haven't pressed the issue yet, though maybe I'll have to—I want to apologize to him because he got hurt to protect me.

We hear the music first, a lively tune played on a fiddle with many voices joining in. Then the orange glow of the torches—so much stronger than the diffuse glow of the lanterns—announces we are getting close. Steagor puts out an arm before we round a bend in the corridor, stopping me. He peers around the corner and only then waves me forward, as if he expects someone to jump out at me at any moment.

I haven't commented on his overprotectiveness, not wanting to bring up bad feelings for him. He has been dealing with some guilt of his own because he thinks he should have been present when Vark and I were attacked. No matter how many times I tell him he wasn't to blame, he is still convinced he shouldn't have left his post.

Maybe I need to find both males together and force them to sit and have an honest conversation with me. And while we're at it, bring in Gorvor and his brother, who is still being held in the Hill, not exactly a prisoner because his room is comfortable enough, yet definitely not free.

But tonight is not the right time. Tonight, we welcome orcs and humans from all over our kingdom and celebrate another successful harvest.

I step into the light and pause, grinning. The great hall has never looked more inviting. Mara and I have planned the event to the last detail, and we commandeered a group of maids and warriors to help us hang garlands from the ceiling and place bushels of apples and pumpkins around the place to make it festive. The flags carrying the black bear emblem hang by the entrances, celebrating our clan.

I find Gorvor with my gaze. He's seated at our table, and he's staring at me with such heat, I flush despite the distance between us. I thank my guards for bringing me here and dismiss them for the night—they should be allowed to enjoy the dinner and the party as much as everyone else.

I make my way through the crowd, greeting everyone I pass. With every step, I feel the king's gaze on me, and I purposefully meander a little more, prolonging the moment. It's a slow dance of seduction, meant only for us. From the corner of my eye, I keep watching him, too. He accepts compliments from the chief of one of the villages and greets the farmers from another settlement. He brings his cup to his lips and takes a long swallow of mead, but all the while, his focus is on me.

I grow damp between my legs as I stop to chat with the herbalist, who takes one look at my full breasts and lifts one eyebrow in a questioning manner. I give her a quick nod and promise to come see her that week. She will be able to help me with any questions I have about the baby I'm carrying—one who will come into this world with green skin and a strong set of lungs, if the other babies I've seen around here are any indication.

By the time I make it to our table, my breathing is out of control, and I want to drag the king back to our bedroom and make love to him all night. This celebration can't be more important than our mate bond, can it?

He grabs me by the wrist and tugs me closer the moment I come within his reach. "Hello, little mate. You are beautiful tonight."

My grin is wide when I answer, "And you look very handsome, my lord."

He growls and yanks me to him, hauling me into his lap. He completely disregards the fact that some kind soul has placed a second carved chair at the big table for me.

"You sit here," he murmurs in my ear.

"You'll hear no complaints from me." I melt against his chest and lift my hands to his shoulders. "Thank you for the lights in the corridors. They are wonderful."

Gorvor grumbles in reply, then leans down and kisses me, invading my mouth with his hot tongue. His warm palms land on my ass, and he brings me closer, rubbing me lightly up and down to let me feel his erection. It strains thick and hard behind the laces of his leather pants.

"I've been wanting you," he rumbles. "And you made me wait even longer."

Only the rumbling of my stomach keeps me in place. If I wasn't so hungry, I'd get up right now, grab Gorvor's hand, and drag him from the hall, propriety be damned.

But my mate chuckles and hands me a plate filled with the best delicacies the cook and the kitchen staff have prepared for tonight. Mixed among the known food are items that the guests have brought, and I try a little bit of everything as orcs come by our table to greet us and talk to their king.

Speeches are an important part of every orc ceremony, including one from Gorvor in which he compliments his people and thanks them for helping with keeping our kingdom prosperous and safe. Orcs cheer, lifting their goblets of mead, and more music follows, with people bursting into song here and there. Some couples stand and start dancing, and others encourage them by clapping loudly and thumping their feet.

It's a happy celebration of a season that was both bountiful and hard, happy and dangerous. But we all made it through, and we needed this evening to acknowledge it.

After a particularly lively dance, Vark steps up to the table and bows to us. His left eye is still covered with a bandage, but his right is as sharp as ever.

I sit forward in Gorvor's lap, smiling at him. "Vark! I'm so glad you could join us."

His skin turns a shade grayer, and he keeps his gaze on the platter in front of us. "My lady. My king."

Biting my lip, I glance back at Gorvor. I don't know what to do with this taciturn Vark, so different from the flirtatious and happy male who used to guard me so well.

The king leans his elbow on the armrest of his throne and asks, "Have you come to tell me you are ready to resume your duties? I am glad."

Vark clenches his jaw, then visibly forces himself to relax. He raises his chin higher and says, "I would like to be reassigned."

My belly twists with an unpleasant sensation. "What? Why?"

He darts a gaze my way, then focuses on Gorvor behind me. "I've failed you. So I would like to resign my post as the queen's guard and make myself useful elsewhere."

"You didn't fail me," I begin. "You almost gave your life to save me, Vark, and I don't—"

Gorvor squeezes my knee and lets out a thoughtful hum. I cut off my flood of words, glancing anxiously between the two men.

"Is that what you want to do?" the king asks Vark.

The warrior dips his chin in a nod. "Aye, my king."

"Very well." Gorvor releases my knee and brushes his

hand over it, soothing. "Report to Ozork tomorrow. He will give you your new assignment."

With a deep bow, Vark departs. He doesn't look back at me, and he leaves the great hall without talking to anyone else.

I turn to Gorvor and widen my eyes. "What was that? You're just letting him go?"

His palm strokes up and down my back, and he seems thoughtful, almost sad.

"Would you have him stay on as your guard even though he doesn't want it?" he asks quietly.

"I— No, of course not," I stammer, taken aback. "But he's clearly going through something, and he's avoiding talking about it."

"And forcing him to return to his post would solve this?"

His lips quirk up in a small smile, but I don't think he's making fun of me. He's giving me the bigger picture.

I cross my arms over my chest. "No," I answer sullenly. "But I hate seeing him so defeated."

Gorvor squeezes my hip. "He will return once he works out what he wants to do. I don't believe he will be gone for long."

I bite my lip, worrying about the big warrior. But the king is right. Vark needs to get through this on his own. I only hope he knows we're here to help if he needs us.

I glance over at Steagor and Neekar. Their watchful gazes scan the crowd, though they're more relaxed than I've seen them in a long time. I hope they'll stay on in our ranks, but at the same time, I wish they found their own mates as well. Now that I understand how much Gorvor has craved what we have, I want everyone to experience the same.

More guests come to the king's table to talk to us, to offer gifts and receive counsel, to report on new births and deaths, or to announce new matings. Gorvor listens to each and every one of them with complete attention, and I do my best to remember the people, their names, and their occupations, because I want to be as good a queen as he is a king.

When orcs return to their tables at last and focus on their food, Gorvor settles me back in his lap and leans his chin on top of my head.

"I love you, little mate," he says quietly.

Heat rises in my cheeks, and I kiss the exposed sliver of green skin at his neck. "I love you, too."

He brings his arms around me, and his hand brushes my sensitive breast. I shiver but don't react, thinking he did it by accident. But when he presses his palm over my core, cupping me through the fabric, I gasp, flushing harder.

"Gorvor, there are *people* here. We can't—"

"Look around, Dawn," he says, his voice burning with intensity.

He turns me in his lap and settles my ass over his hard cock. His hand traces my belly, the heat of it seeping through my dress and shift. I'm too distracted at first to know what he means, but once I focus my gaze on what's going on, I still, observing the orcs below us.

One by one, the torches in the great hall are dimmed, creating a sultry, intimate atmosphere. Elderly orcs lead the children out by various exits, and adolescents follow, dragging their feet. On a low stage, performers are setting up their act, the musicians and actors warming up to give the orc king and his court some entertainment. Noise rises in the underground dome, echoes multiplying the sounds of conversation and the clinking of cups and dishes.

Gorvor's hand skims up, and he cups my breast, squeezing. In the dim light of the great hall, his movements are half concealed, and for once, no one is looking at us. Instead, all eyes are trained on the performers...only that's not entirely true. The show is there only for the background, but the orcs are intent on each other, tension rising in the room.

The king pinches my nipple, and I gasp, instinctively rocking my hips back. My ass meets his thick cock. A shiver runs through me, my nipples drawing into stiff, sensitive points. I love it when he worships my body, but we've never done anything quite so...public.

We're definitely not the only ones in the room succumbing to the languid, seductive atmosphere created by the low drums and flickering torchlight. An orc male disappears under his partner's skirts, and she leans back on the table, eyes closed in bliss. A human man braces his arms on the wall while his orc lover grinds his hips into him from behind, both still clothed but probably not for long.

"What's going on?" I whisper, tilting my head to the side to catch Gorvor's gaze.

His grin is feral, his eyes glimmering with heat. "It's a harvest festival."

"What does that mean?"

I can't resist peeking at a trio of orcs, all in various stages of undress, kissing, licking, touching.

"We plant our seed tonight," Gorvor murmurs against my neck, then presses a hot kiss to my skin.

"Our seed—*oh!*" The realization dawns on me, and I shudder from excitement. "Really?"

"It's our way to thank the gods for the harvest." He kisses his way up my neck, his tusks adding to the sensation. "And make sure the next year is fertile as well."

Orcs aren't self-conscious about sex and their bodies, that much I've learned already, but it's one thing to know something and another thing entirely to experience it first-hand.

Yet I'm not shrinking away. Gorvor inches up the skirts of my dress with one hand while his other is still at my breast, teasing my nipple through the fabric.

"Gorvor," I whisper. "A-are you sure?"

He hums behind me, and the sound reverberates inside me, sparking off my too-tight nerves. "You will like it, little mate."

"And if I don't?" I insist, though my voice grows breathier with every caress.

He grabs my chin with one hand and turns me halfway around so I'm forced to look him in his eyes. "Then I will stop."

I let out a shuddering exhale. That was all I needed to know. "All right."

A flash of warm approval enters his gaze, and he kisses me, licking into my mouth with his hot, talented tongue. I whimper and cling to him, urgency rising inside me now he has promised me safety. A low groan echoes through the room from someone who has clearly found pleasure. But I don't glance around to see who it is. I only have eyes for my mate.

Suddenly, he tears himself from the kiss and shifts me on his lap so I'm facing away from him again. With movements that border on rough, he yanks my knees apart, so I'm spread completely, and anchors me against his chest with one massive arm. If I wasn't wearing a dress, I'd be obscenely spread out for anyone to see, and the thought of it has my pussy growing wet.

Only with Gorvor have I ever felt this way.

Now he reaches under my dress, rucking up the silk in a seductive rustle. Anyone looking at us would know what we're doing immediately, but I'm covered enough that I'm not on display for anyone, and neither is the king.

The thrill of it only adds to my arousal.

Nothing in my life has prepared me for this moment. But I want it. I don't know what I'd do if Gorvor threw me on the table and fucked me there in front of everyone, like another male is doing to his mate at the other end of the hall. She clearly enjoys it, her moans mingling with the rising voices of the others who are participating in this fertility ritual.

Would I tell him to stop, to let me go? Or scream my pleasure out loud for all the hall to hear?

His thick, warm fingers skim up my thigh, and I hold my breath, gritting my teeth so I don't cry out the moment he reaches my core. But the evil orc doesn't go straight for the prize. With clever touches, he drives me wild, tracing the seam of my leg and the softness of my inner thighs, all the while nuzzling my neck, giving me little biting kisses that soon have me panting in his arms.

Right when I'm about to demand more, he finally slips his fingers to my pussy, easily parting me. He growls a rough curse, his big body tensing all around me. He pulls me tighter against his chest, and I deliberately roll my hips over his heavy cock, teasing as much as I can in return.

"Wicked," he murmurs in my ear. "When you walked up to me that first day, all dirty and defiant, I never dreamed I would get to have you like this."

Without warning, he presses a calloused pad of his forefinger on my pearl and flicks it, hard. My back bows in pleasure, and I bite my lip to keep a yelp from escaping.

"You're so wet for me," he purrs. "You're perfect. I'll fill you up, and you'll ride me in front of everyone."

"Yes," I gasp. "I need you."

Gorvor curses again, and a moment later, he lifts me easily with one arm while he fumbles with his laces. Then the bare backs of my thighs meet his naked skin, and I know this is it. I could stop him. But I need this more than I need my next breath.

He hooks his hands beneath my legs, and I reach between us to grasp his cock. It's hot and thick, the broad green head already slick with precum, and I smear it all over, readying him for me. The bulging knot at the bottom pulses with heat, and I wonder, as I always seem to do, if it'll fit, if my body was made for this.

But Gorvor is already lowering me, so I hold his cock firm and notch it in place. The first push through my slick pussy is always a shock, the stretch almost too much. He doesn't give me time to reconsider. Gravity takes hold, and I slide down his thickness, inch by inch, until my ass meets his groin.

Gorvor's rough exhale over my bare neck is the only sign that he's as affected by this as I am. I palm the back of his head, running my fingers through his silky hair. And when he digs his fingers into my thighs and lifts me again, then jerks me down, I dig my nails into his neck, holding on.

The sensation of being so full is incredible. I writhe in Gorvor's arms to make him speed up his movements, but he doesn't obey. He fucks me slowly, keeping his hands on my waist so he controls the rhythm. Every push of his thick cock through my aching pussy brings me closer to bliss, and I hold on as best I can, closing my eyes at the sensations coursing through me.

Then he buries one hand back under my skirts and finds my pearl with his fingers. The first brush of his rough pad over the sensitive spot has me crying out. I clap my hand over my mouth, horrified at the thought of the others hearing me.

But Gorvor nips the side of my neck and growls, "Don't hold back. Let them hear you. Let them hear how well I'm fucking you."

His words release something in my chest, and I grow wetter in a rush, taking Gorvor all the way to his knot, which pushes rudely at my pussy every time he drags me down over his length. His fingers at my center strum that delicate part of me, and I give myself over to the moment, relaxing my muscles.

"Gorvor," I whisper. "I'm pregnant."

The words slip from my mouth, a confession I'd meant to save for later. But even though we're in the presence of so many others, this moment is so intimate. It's about us, enjoying each other's bodies, loving and safe.

My mate stills behind me, and I feel the thundering beat of his heart at my back.

"Are you sure?" he rasps.

I bite my lip and nod quickly.

His massive body shudders, then he grasps my chin and turns my head to the side. He kisses me roughly, until I'm whimpering with desire. I clench my inner muscles around his cock, so close to coming but unable to tumble over the edge.

At last, he pulls back and looks right into my eyes. "You have given me the most beautiful gift, my mate."

I smile, unable to stem the flow of happy tears. "And you to me."

Gorvor grins, then wraps his arms around me and reaches under my skirts again. "I'm going to make you come so hard, Dawn. Over and over again, and then I'll bring you gifts and food." He rocks me over his cock in a renewed rhythm, each thrust gaining in strength. "You won't want for anything."

"I know," I pant. "You always take care of me."

He presses down on my sensitive button, and I shatter, screaming in bliss. I slide farther down, taking Gorvor's knot, and he pumps faster until he bellows, his head thrown back. Jets of liquid heat fill me, and the pulsing of his knot triggers another climax, until we collapse back on the throne together, sweaty and sated.

Slowly, reality intrudes on our happy little bubble. I become aware of the great hall around us, of the orcs fucking and kissing and dancing without a care in the world. I'm sure some of them saw and heard us, but they don't care—this festival is about giving and receiving pleasure, the most natural thing in the world.

"I knew you would like it," Gorvor mutters, his expression smug. "My mate has come to enjoy the orc ways."

"I had a wonderful teacher," I say, leaning back against his warm chest. "The best."

He smooths my skirts over us, giving us privacy. The knot locks us together, and we remain in place, content to watch the performance for a while. Then I squeeze my inner muscles again, and he groans, his chuckle more than a little strained.

"If you want to be let off my cock anytime soon," he rumbles in my ear, "you'd better behave."

I bite my lip and squeeze him again, and he hisses, then takes my shoulders and pushes them forward, guiding me to brace my hands against the massive wood table still spread with the remains of our feast. Gorvor runs his palm over my back, and I send him a wicked grin over my shoulder. He knows exactly what I want, and he will always give it to me.

His smile is feral as he says, "Hold on, little mate."

The End

~

Thank you so much for reading Dawn and Gorvor's story! I hope you enjoyed it.

I wrote you a bonus epilogue - from Gorvor's point of view! So if you want to know what he felt the moment he first saw Dawn *and* see how things are going for this awesome couple in a few months, download the bonus scene today! If you're reading this in paperback or can't access the link, email me at zoe@zoeashwood.com.

And if you want Steagor's story, you can read it today - *Her Orc Guardian* will take you back to the Black Bear Hill.

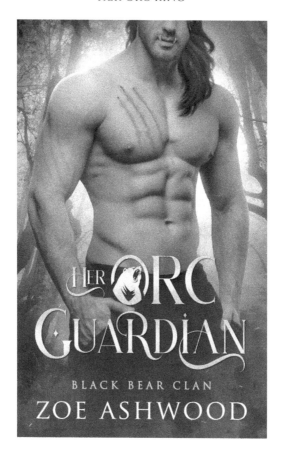

And here's a completely **free novella** with a full happy ending for you! Download Her Orc Mate now or email me at zoe@zoeashwood.com if you can't access the link!

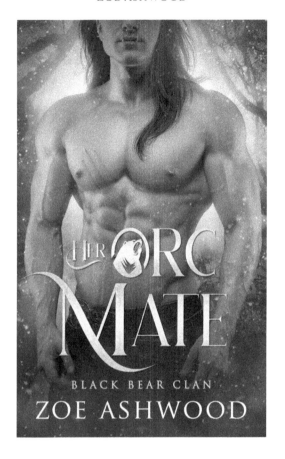

I hope you'll keep returning to this world.

xo, Zoe

ALSO BY ZOE ASHWOOD

BLACK BEAR CLAN

(orc fantasy romance)

Her Orc Mate - freebie!

Her Orc King

Her Orc Guardian

Her Orc Warrior

Her Orc Protector

Her Orc Husband

Her Orc Gentleman

NORSE SEA DRAGONS duet

(Paranormal Romance, complete)

Deep Sea Kiss

Deep Sea Love

ICE PLANET RENDU

(Sfi-Fi Alien Romance, complete)

Cold Attraction

Cold Temptation

Cold Seduction

SEA DRAGONS OF AMBER BAY

(Reverse Harem Romance, complete)

Tempted

Ensnared

Seduced

NORA MOSS

(Reverse Harem Romance, complete)

Jinxed in Love, freebie

Cursed in Love

Captured in Love

Freed in Love

SHIFT SERIES

(Paranormal Romance)

Bearly Married, freebie

Trust the Wolf

Truth or Bear

Make Him Howl

Acknowledgments

This book was such a joy to write. Sometimes, books take a lot of energy to power through, but this one didn't - the characters popped onto the page fully formed, their story clear in my head. I love it when that happens!

I'm grateful to some amazing women who helped me bring this story idea into the world - either by encouraging me and doing word sprints with me or by offering advice and helping me polish my prose. I'm a lucky author to have a support crew so awesome, and coworkers who get me.

A big thank you to you, dear reader, for trusting me enough to take the leap into this orc romance world with me! I'm grateful for every single book you read because that allows me to do what I love most as a real job. I have so many cool books planned, yay!

I'd like to also say thank you to my family, who pull me away from the keyboard and into adventures of our own. It's through our family hikes and forest walks that I envisioned the orc kingdom! Big thanks to my husband, the love of my life, and to our boys, who force me to see the world with fresh eyes. And last but not least, a big smooch to our dog, who demands daily walks and loves to sprawl out next to my desk, sleeping while I do the hard work.

Every day, I'm grateful that I get to do this writing thing for a living. It's a dream come true!

xo, Zoe

ABOUT THE AUTHOR

Zoe Ashwood writes sexy paranormal romance for women who believe in magic and true love.

While she's always been a reader, Zoe's writing used to be limited to diary scribbles and bad (really *bad*) teenage poetry. Then she participated in NaNoWriMo 2015 and never looked back.

She's happily married to her best friend and has two boys who are as stubborn as they're cute and a very fluffy dog.

She's always super happy to hear from fellow bookworms, so don't hesitate to get in touch! Her newsletter is an especially great way to stay up-to-date with all the latest news (and get a free book). Or you can catch up with her in her Facebook group!